STEPHEN DANDO-COLLINS

CAESAR

the war dog

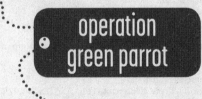

operation
green parrot

RANDOM HOUSE AUSTRALIA

A Random House book
Published by Random House Australia Pty Ltd
Level 3, 100 Pacific Highway, North Sydney NSW 2060
www.randomhouse.com.au

First published by Random House Australia in 2015

Addresses for companies within the Random House Group can be found at
www.randomhouse.com.au/offices

National Library of Australia
Cataloguing-in-Publication Entry

Author: Dando-Collins, Stephen
Title: Caesar the war dog: operation green parrot/Stephen Dando-Collins
ISBN: 9 780 85798 471 5 (pbk)
Series: Caesar the war dog; 4
Target audience: For primary school age.
Subjects: Dogs – Juvenile fiction.
    Detector dogs – Juvenile fiction.
    Kidnapping – Juvenile fiction.
Dewey number: A823.3

Cover photographs: dog © Ruth O'Leary/ruthlessphotos.com; background © JeniFoto/
Shutterstock; Apache helicopters © vadimmmus/Shutterstock
Cover design by Astred Hicks, designcherry
Typeset by Midland Typesetters, Australia
Printed in Australia by Griffin Press, an accredited ISO AS/NZS 14001:2004
Environmental Management System printer

Random House Australia uses papers that are natural, renewable and recyclable
products and made from wood grown in sustainable forests. The logging and
manufacturing processes are expected to conform to the environmental
regulations of the country of origin.

*Once again for Louise, who shares Caesar's adventures
with me from the first glimmer of an idea to
the very last correction. With grateful thanks to
Richard, Zoe and Catriona, and to the
many readers who tell me how much they love
Caesar the war dog and can't wait
until his next adventure.*

CHAPTER 1

The President of the United States gazed down the line of thirteen soldiers standing to rigid attention. Hailing from seven different countries, all of them wore the varying uniforms of their national armies, except for one item of apparel they had in common – the sky-blue beret of the United Nations. The President dropped his eyes to the chocolate labrador sitting dutifully beside one of the soldiers. The dog, wearing the red parade vest of the EDD section of the Australian Army's Special Operations Engineer Regiment (SOER), stared directly ahead, just like the soldiers around him, in best military fashion.

'So, this is the famous Caesar the war dog,' said the President. He was a tall, handsome man with greying hair. 'Maybe I should just give the award to him, seeing he's the only member of this top-secret United Nations unit who's permitted to be named and photographed.'

Everyone laughed, and the President excused himself to walk over to the lectern. He proceeded to deliver

1

a speech praising the UN's Global Rapid Reaction Responders (GRRR) for the work they had done from Afghanistan to Africa and places in between.

'I understand you have come here direct from an operation in the Caribbean,' he went on, 'where you rescued the Belgian Ambassador to the United States and his family from modern-day pirates. The fact that, for reasons of international security, this operation was kept out of the media and officially never happened, in no way lessens the importance of your work and dedicated service. You are volunteers and, wherever you are in the world, you are prepared to drop whatever you are doing to defuse a crisis situation – at great risk to yourselves – which deserves enormous credit. This citation is well earned.'

Stepping down from the dais to applause, the President turned to a United States Marine Corps sergeant holding a scroll upon a red velvet cushion.

'Captain Lee,' he called, taking the scroll, 'please step forward.'

Liberty Lee, Commander of GRRR, stepped forward. She came stiffly to attention in front of the President and saluted.

'Captain,' said the President, 'I'm pleased that you and your team were able to drop by to see us here in Washington prior to their returning to base.'

'Yes, sir,' replied Liberty.

'On behalf of the people and the government of the United States, it gives me great pleasure to present the Global Rapid Reaction Responders with the Presidential Unit Citation, which has rarely been awarded to non-American military units.' He handed the scroll to Liberty.

'Thank you, Mr President.' Liberty accepted the citation scroll and stiffly saluted once more. 'It is a great honour. This award will be proudly displayed at UN headquarters.'

Soon, the official ceremony was over and the President moved along the line of GRRR members, talking to each one in turn, with Captain Lee providing introductions. First to receive the President's attention was Sergeant Charlie Grover, VC, of the Australian Army's Special Air Service Regiment, the famous and elite SAS. Next was a diminutive trooper from the SAS known to friend and foe alike as Bendigo Baz, followed by three American Special Forces soldiers – the gum-chewing Sergeant Duke Hazard, Texan Sergeant Tim McHenry and signaller Corporal Brian Cisco. Direct from the UK were Scotsman Sergeant Angus Bruce of the Royal Marine Commandos, and Corporal Chris Banner of the Special Boat Service.

The President then chatted to Sergeant Jean-Claude Lyon from the French Foreign Legion, Corporal Casper Mortenson from the Danish Army's Hunter Corps, and combat medic Private Willy Wolf from the German Army's Kommando Spezialkräfte. And from the Japanese Self-Defence Force, there was Corporal Toushi Harada, the unit's computer whiz. When the President reached Toushi and held out his hand, Toushi bowed to him. Last of all, the President came to Caesar and his handler, Sergeant Ben Fulton of the Australian Army's SOER.

'I saved you for last, Caesar,' said the President, grinning cheekily.

Caesar responded by holding up one paw.

Laughing, the President bent and shook the paw as if he were shaking a hand. Then the leader of the free world straightened and waved an aide forward. The aide, dressed in a smart white uniform, carried a silver plate upon which sat a large bone.

'I figured that Caesar would appreciate a juicy bone more than a citation,' the President said to Ben, 'so I asked the White House's executive chef to rustle up something special for him. Is it okay if I give it to Caesar, Sergeant?'

'Sure is, sir,' Ben responded proudly. 'Can't be many dogs that get to have a bone presented to them by the President of the United States himself. My kids, Josh and Maddie, won't believe it!'

'You're right,' the President said. 'The only other canines with that privilege are my family's two pet dogs.'

He nodded to the aide, who took the bone from the plate and placed it on the grass in front of Caesar.

With his tail wagging, the brown labrador lowered his nose and sniffed the bone. Then he looked up at Ben, as if asking, *Can I have it, boss?*

Ben broke into a smile. 'That's okay, mate,' he said to his four-legged partner. 'Go ahead and enjoy the bone. I think we can trust the White House kitchen staff not to poison you.'

Caesar eased down and, holding the bone in place with his right paw, began to gnaw at it.

The President's brow creased with surprise. 'You mean to say that people have tried to give your dog poisoned bones before today, Sergeant?'

'Oh, yes, sir,' Ben replied. 'In Afghanistan, Caesar and war dogs like him became such a threat to the Taliban, they tried leaving poisoned food out for them. But Caesar is very good about stray food. He will usually ask me if it's okay to eat something.'

'That is how intelligent this dog is, sir,' said Liberty Lee.

'More intelligent than many human, sir,' added Toushi.

The President chuckled. 'I can believe it.'

'He has saved all our lives at one time or another, Mr President,' said Liberty earnestly. 'There's no EDD that compares to Caesar. GRRR would not be the same without him.'

'Caesar is a good name,' said the President, nodding to himself. 'Very military. Did you name him, Sergeant?'

Ben shook his head. 'No, sir. He'd been given that name by the time I came across him in the training kennels.'

'You know, there was a United States Marine Corps dog served in Bougainville in the Pacific during the Second World War which, I do believe, also had the name of Caesar.'

'I didn't know that, sir,' replied Ben.

'So, where do you folks go from here?' the President asked.

'Most of us will return to our regular units, sir, until GRRR is needed again,' Ben answered. 'As for Sergeant Grover, Caesar and myself, we're heading for the University of Texas to speak at a police seminar on rapid response.'

'I'm guessing that Caesar won't actually be speaking at the conference,' the President said with a grin.

Ben smiled. 'Oh, I'm sure Caesar will be showing police from all over America a few of his EDD tricks, sir.'

'I'd like to see that. So, where in Texas exactly are you headed?'

'San Antonio, sir.'

The President looked pleased. 'San Antonio? That's a mighty fine city. They have a champion NBA team and the best rodeo in the country.' He leaned in closer to

Ben. 'And of course it's home to the Alamo. You should check it out if you get a chance. Believe me, you won't forget your time in San Antonio.'

CHAPTER 2

The hot Texan sun glinted off the closely shaven head of Antonio Lopez. Kneeling at the low brick wall that skirted the rooftop, and using binoculars, he studied San Antonio's slow-moving downtown traffic. His attention was focused on a late-model Chevrolet Impala sedan being towed away, six storeys below.

'Boom!' he said with a faint smile. 'And El Loro Verde's brother will be dead, just like that, with one little car bomb. Clever, huh, Manny?'

'*Sí*, Antonio. But how much longer before we can vamoose?' grumbled his associate Emanuel 'Manny' Diaz.

'Until I say we can,' Lopez said firmly. 'So, keep writing what I tell you when I tell you.' He checked his watch, noting the exact time.

'Okay, *Patrón*,' Manny replied with a sigh.

Lopez returned the binoculars to his eyes. 'So, we have established that a stolen automobile can be parked in the street for three hours before the city authorities tow it away. *Sí*?'

'*Sí*, three hours.'

'Now, the traffic signals. They change –' Lopez paused, then checked his watch again – 'every two minutes.'

'The traffic signals, they change every two minutes,' Manny acknowledged, scribbling on a notepad.

'Okay, now we'll see how the cops react.' Laying aside his binoculars, Lopez took out a phone and dialled 911.

'Emergency,' answered a female voice. 'What service do you require?'

'Quick! Get me the police!' Lopez said with fake urgency. 'I see a man with a gun.'

Moments later, a male voice came on the line. 'San Antonio Police Department.'

'There is a man with a gun – a rifle,' said Lopez. 'I think he is going to shoot some people. Corner of East Houston and Broadway.'

'Can I have your name, sir?'

Lopez ignored the question. 'You must hurry! The man is wearing a long blue coat and a baseball cap. He is outside the bank, north side of the intersection of East Houston and Broadway. You must hurry, or something bad will happen.' Lopez hung up.

The two men waited. A few minutes passed before they heard the approach of police sirens. Lopez trained his binoculars on the corner of East Houston Street and Broadway, opposite. Before long, a pair of police motorcycles slew to a halt. The policemen dismounted and, drawing their Smith & Wesson M&P40 revolvers, took cover behind parked cars. Lopez could see them calling and waving to pedestrians, urging them to get off the pavement. They then levelled their revolvers at a man sitting on the footpath with his back to the wall of the Texas National Bank building.

The man appeared to have only one leg and was wearing a baseball cap, a long overcoat, jeans and dark glasses. A rug on the pavement in front of him was littered with small change and a few dollar notes. A handmade cardboard sign suspended around his neck read 'Vietnam Vet. I gave. How about you?' Two metal objects lay beside him; from a distance they looked the length and size of a rifle.

More wailing sirens rent the air. Within minutes, police cars were pulling up with screeching tyres north, south, east and west of the intersection. Armed police officers tumbled out and took up firing positions, aiming at the man on the pavement.

Lopez checked his watch. 'Just over four minutes,' he said.

Below, police dashed toward the seated man. He raised his hands, protesting vehemently, but was roughly bundled over onto his chest, frisked and then hand-cuffed. The policemen soon realised that the objects lying beside the man were crutches, not rifles. If he were to walk anywhere, the man needed his hands free to use his crutches. He was lifted to a standing position, freed from the handcuffs and handed the crutches.

As he was escorted away to a police car, to be taken to headquarters for questioning, the man loudly protested that he'd only been begging for money. He added that some shiny-headed Hispanic guy he'd never seen before had paid him fifty bucks to sit on that particular corner. With the traffic stopped, Lopez and his offsider could hear the one-legged man's protests from all the way up on the roof across the street. Lopez was grinning.

'What now, *Patrón*?' asked Manny.

'Now we wait to see if our friend Marron keeps his regular appointment. Come, out of the sun.' Lopez rose and, with his subordinate following close behind, led the way to the rooftop stairwell, where they would hide, out of sight.

🐾🐾

Thirty minutes later, the two Mexican gunmen scuttled across the rooftop to their previous viewing position. Kneeling at the low brick wall, Lopez checked his watch: ten minutes before noon. Lopez held the binoculars to his eyes once more, focused on the entrance to the Texas National Bank.

A clock in the distance began to chime. A black Chrysler 300C drew to a halt outside the bank. Twenty-two-year-old, curly headed Rocky Marron emerged from a rear door of the sedan. He was wearing an expensive business suit, white T-shirt, sunglasses and a San Antonio Spurs baseball cap. He looked up and down the street warily. Seemingly satisfied with what he saw, Marron took a suitcase from the Chrysler's back seat and hurried to the bank's revolving door. As soon as he was inside the building, the sedan took off up the street.

Lopez nodded to himself as he removed the binoculars from his eyes. 'Every Tuesday and Wednesday, precisely at noon, Rocky arrives to make a deposit. A creature of habit, our friend Rocky. To stay alive, he should change the pattern of his behaviour.'

'His habit will be the death of him!' Manny said with a smile.

Lopez turned for the stairs. 'Take me to the bomb-maker. Tomorrow we shall return to give Rocky Marron an explosive welcome when he comes to make his next deposit.'

CHAPTER 3

Late that afternoon, a captain and a sergeant from the San Antonio Police Department met Ben, Caesar and Charlie at Lackland Air Force Base on the western outskirts of San Antonio. The US Air Force had laid on a ride for the Aussies in a Hercules C-130 that had been winging its way down from Washington on a routine transport flight. Flying in a Hercules was as normal as breathing to Caesar, Ben and Charlie. Caesar's tail had started wagging furiously as he was led toward the big transport plane at Andrews Base in Washington. Seeing the Herc, Caesar had thought they must be going for a parachute jump – an activity he loved.

'Over here, you guys,' called the SAPD's Captain Leo De Silva. He and his companion stood beside a black-and-white station wagon with 'POLICE, Protecting the Alamo City' painted on its side. The Alamo, it seemed to the Australian visitors, was a big deal here.

Ben and Charlie waved as they emerged from a terminal building. Both men had their military kitbag slung over a shoulder and made their way over with Caesar trotting along beside them on a two-metre metal leash.

'Leo De Silva,' said the police captain, extending his hand to Charlie. He was tall and olive-skinned, with a thick moustache adorning his top lip. 'And this is Sergeant "Tex" Austin.' Austin was shorter, dumpier and losing his hair.

There were handshakes all round.

'Call me Charlie.'

'I'm Ben Fulton, and this is Caesar,' said Ben.

De Silva nodded toward the station wagon's rear hatch. 'Caesar can go in the back with the bags.'

'I'd rather Caesar rode inside with me, sir,' replied Ben. 'He could get hurt rolling around in the back.'

The police captain raised his eyebrows. 'Okay.'

'You sure you don't want the dawg to drive while we're at it?' Sergeant Austin said in a supercilious tone.

'Caesar only drives in emergencies,' said Charlie, keeping a straight face.

Austin looked at him with surprise, before breaking into a grin.

The two Americans climbed into the front while Ben and Charlie sat in the back with Caesar between them. The station wagon was soon speeding southwest along the highway toward downtown San Antonio.

'So, when we were in Washington, the President said we should check out the Alamo while we're down here,' said Ben. 'What's that all about?'

'You've never heard of the Alamo?' said an incredulous Captain De Silva.

'Can't say that I have.'

'Partner, it's only the most famous historic battle site in Texas, if not in all of America. In 1836, Jim Bowie, Davy Crockett and a bunch of Texans occupied the Alamo, an old Spanish mission, while they held off the whole Mexican army of General Santa Anna. They did it for close to two weeks. Outnumbered fifteen to one, they were. They ended up all falling, fighting for Texas's liberty.'

'I remember seeing a movie about it when I was a kid,' said Charlie. 'Jim Bowie invented the Bowie knife, didn't he?'

'That's the guy,' De Silva said proudly.

'And you say the Texans all died in the battle?' Ben asked.

De Silva nodded. 'Uh-huh. The Texans lost the battle but won the war and established the Republic of Texas, before it became a US state. Santa Anna's army was defeated by Sam Houston's Texan army a little while later at San Jacinto. Only took them eighteen minutes to do it. These days, we got our hands full here in San Antonio with the invasion of the Mexican crime cartels.'

'The cartels have a foothold here?' Ben asked, surprised.

'More than a foothold. If you drive south for five or six hours, you'll be in Monterrey, the crime capital of Mexico. With more than half the population of San Antonio being Hispanic, and a lot of those folks having relatives in Mexico, it was pretty natural that the crime bosses would set up operations here, too. The Mexican Government is at war with those crime cartels – has been for years – and that war spills over into Texas all the time.'

'You have your hands full, then,' said Charlie.

'Well, things aren't out of hand here the way they are in Monterrey and other parts of the Mexican border states. But take it from me, guys, the Mexican cartels will stop at nothing. When they're not fighting the police and the military, they're fighting each other.'

'How many Mexican cartels are there?' asked Ben.

'At last count, thirty-seven. And some of those cartels have thousands of people on their payrolls. The Mexican police are outnumbered by them. And the cartels used to be better-armed than the police. That's why the Mexican Government brought their military into the fight against crime a few years back.'

'Who's winning?' asked Charlie.

'The Mexican Government has won back some control. But, like I say, there's a war going on south of the border. IEDs have become a key part of the cartels' weapons inventory.' De Silva turned and looked at Caesar. 'That's why the seminar with your famous EDD has sold out. Everyone wants to have an edge on the bad guys when it comes to bombs. And a dawg as versatile as yours seems to represent that edge, Ben.'

'Well, Caesar and I are happy to share our expertise, sir.'

De Silva and Austin dropped the Australian trio off at a University of Texas accommodation wing in downtown San Antonio, arranging to collect them the next morning and take them to the seminar.

Ben, Caesar and Charlie were met by Mrs Rosario, the superintendent of the university's on-site accommodation. She was a tiny woman with bright red hair.

'What a handsome dog you have,' she said, smiling at the brown labrador with the wagging tail.

'This is Caesar, ma'am. I'm Ben and this is Charlie,' Ben said by way of introduction.

Her eyes sparkled. 'César? Why, this is a good Hispanic name. We have a hero here in San Antonio by the same name – César Chávez. He started the United Farm Workers and did great things for the rights of the people working in the fields. To get here, you would have driven along a boulevard named in his honour. Come, I'll show you to your rooms, and where César can sleep.'

'If you don't mind, ma'am, Caesar will sleep with me,' said Ben.

Mrs Rosario looked surprised. 'Such a large dog sleeps with you?'

'On the floor beside my bed. Sometimes he does sneak onto the bed and snuggle up beside me. Don't you, mate?' Ben gave his four-legged companion a vigorous pat. Caesar, his tail wagging furiously, responded by licking him on the cheek.

'I don't agree with dogs in bedrooms,' said the woman.

'This is no ordinary dog, Mrs Rosario,' said Charlie. 'He's more like Ben's son.'

'Is that right?' Mrs Rosario clearly did not approve. 'And what happens when his "son" wants to go to the bathroom?'

'He'll tell me and I'll take him outside,' said Ben. 'Don't worry, I always clean up after him.'

'I see.' The woman didn't sound convinced. 'We have very strict hygiene rules here, you know. This way.'

Inside a garage in a rundown part of west San Antonio, surrounded by armed men with star tattoos on their necks and the backs of their hands, Antonio Lopez and Manny Diaz were inspecting two vehicles – a grey GMC Savana van and a battered 14-seat Toyota minibus. The front and sides of the minibus were emblazoned with the words 'Texian Transit Company' and an image of a big yellow star.

'El Globo, you got the numbers Manny must call tomorrow?'

'Sí, Patrón.' A rotund, middle-aged man removed two small pieces of paper from his pocket. Each had a phone number written on it. 'One for the first bomb. Another for the second.'

'You memorise those numbers, Manny,' Lopez instructed. 'You memorise the numbers good and then you destroy the pieces of paper. Got it?'

'Got it, Patrón,' said Manny. He took the pieces of paper and studied the numbers. 'You can rely on me. Memorise the numbers and destroy the pieces of paper. Simple.'

Lopez looked at him fiercely. 'I am relying on you, *amigo*. Screw up tomorrow, and your little ones will be looking for a new father.'

Manny paled. 'When have I ever let Estrella down, *Patrón*?' He displayed the star tattoo on the back of his right hand. 'My loyalty is more than skin-deep. It is in the blood. There is no lieutenant more faithful in all the world. Trust me, Rocky Marron is as good as dead. It will all go like the workings of a clock.'

Lopez smiled. 'Tick, tock, BOOM!'

CHAPTER 4

At precisely 7.30 am, the San Antonio Police Department's Sergeant Austin collected Ben, Caesar and Charlie to drive them across town.

'Captain De Silva will catch you later at the conference,' the sergeant advised from behind the wheel.

'Where is the conference?' Ben asked.

'The Sheraton Gunter Hotel, one of San Antonio's oldest hotels – and the most haunted.'

'Haunted?' Charlie looked up from the speech he was to deliver. 'I don't believe in ghosts.'

'Is it far?' Ben asked, patting Caesar, who was sitting beside him.

'No, it's in the financial district – just four blocks from the Alamo,' said Austin.

They turned onto East Houston Street and passed a grey van parked outside the Texas National Bank. The Texian Transport minibus was parked only a block away. Both vehicles contained IEDs built around twenty kilograms of C-4 plastic explosive. And both

IEDs were linked to detonation devices designed to be set off when Manny Diaz rang the mobile phones attached to them.

A hotel doorman greeted Ben, Caesar and Charlie when they alighted outside the Sheraton Gunter Hotel. As the trio strode into the lobby, passers-by turned to take in the two soldiers in camouflage uniform and wearing the sky-blue beret of the United Nations. But most of the attention was directed at Caesar, who moved along at Ben's side on his short leash, taking in the sights and smells of the busy five-star hotel.

A grey-haired concierge hurried to greet the new arrivals. 'Good morning. Are you here to attend the conference, gentlemen?' he asked.

'Sergeants G and F, and EDD Caesar,' Charlie announced, shaking the man's hand. 'We are guest speakers at the conference.'

'Yes, sir, we've been expecting you,' said the concierge, resisting the temptation to make a quip about Caesar being a guest speaker who couldn't speak. 'You have asked to check out the conference room in advance?'

'Roger to that,' said Charlie.

'This way, sirs. You will have to go through the metal detector, but that will be a mere formality for you military folks.' Ahead, security personnel waited at a walk-through metal detector similar to the kind used at airports.

As Charlie reached the detector, he turned to the security guard in charge. 'You'll have to take these into account,' he said, then bent down and pulled up his left trouser leg to reveal a Zoomer prosthetic leg. Composed of carbon fibre and various metal parts, it was attached to what was left of his upper left leg after a bloody battle in Afghanistan.

The security guard's eyes widened. 'You serve in the military with a prosthetic leg, Sergeant?'

'No,' Charlie responded with a smile. '*Two* prosthetic legs.' He proceeded to roll up his right trouser leg to show a second, shorter Zoomer attached to his lower right leg.

'Wow!' said the security guard. 'How does that work for you?'

'Pretty well,' said Charlie, before he walked through the scanner.

The metal fittings on his Zoomers set off a high-pitched alarm, and the security guards patted Charlie down to make sure that he wasn't carrying a weapon or explosives into the convention. Charlie rarely travelled with commercial airlines where this sort of security check was the norm. He usually flew on military aircraft and was the one looking after the security of others. Patiently, he raised his arms and allowed the security guards to do their job.

'All clear. Thank you, sir,' said the chief guard.

Next, it was Ben and Caesar's turn to go through the metal detector. Before they did this, Ben had to remove Caesar's collar and leash, which were handed around the detector by the guards. First, Ben instructed Caesar to sit in front of the detector and wait. Ben then walked through without setting off any alarms. All the while, Caesar sat looking intently at Ben, watching and listening for a hand signal, a whistle or a command.

'Isn't he cute?' a passing woman said to her friends, nodding to the obedient labrador.

Caesar barely even heard her. The focus of his attention was on his master.

Ben now turned to Caesar. 'Come on, mate,' he called, patting his thigh.

In an instant, Caesar was up. But instead of going through the metal detector, he skirted around it with a wagging tail and came to sit beside Ben. This brought laughter from the security guards.

'He can't do that, Sergeant,' the chief security guard said with a grin. 'That's cheating. He's got to go through, just like everyone else. Them's the rules.'

'Caesar, go back through,' said Ben, pointing to the detector.

Caesar immediately rose and went trotting through the detector, in the reverse direction. Then he turned and looked at Ben, his head to one side, as if to say, *Now what, boss?*

'Come back through, mate,' Ben instructed, waving him forward.

Caesar did so, receiving a pat from Ben on the other side. Ben fixed Caesar's collar back in place, and they continued down the corridor with Charlie to the main conference room, where they were met by the manager of the conference. The room was set up like a theatre, with row upon row of chairs, and a dais and lectern up the front. Projected on a massive screen behind the dais were the title of the conference – the North American Rapid Response Conference – and its flash logo.

Ben unclipped the leash from Caesar's collar. 'Seek on, Caesar,' he instructed. 'Seek on!' He pointed to the left side of the conference room. 'Start this side, with the back row. Let's go, boy!'

With his nose to the ground, Caesar launched into a search for explosives. Ben directed him along row after row of empty chairs, and after several minutes they completed a thorough sweep of the entire room without finding anything suspicious.

'What a goose I would have looked if we hadn't checked the room and there was something planted here,' Ben said to the manager as he snapped Caesar's leash back in place.

'We have another sniffer dog on the program tomorrow,' said the manager. 'He's not famous like your Caesar, of course. This dog works in the local prisons, sniffing for the lithium found in mobile-phone batteries. Prisoners sneak the phones in to run crime from their cells, or to organise prison breaks.'

'Lithium?' Ben nodded. 'Yes, you can train a dog to track down just about any scent. But a good war dog like Caesar does a whole lot more than track scents.'

Caesar's usual reward for a job well done was nothing more than a solid pat and an encouraging word from his master. Ben didn't favour food rewards because a dog that always receives food rewards was bound to get fat. And a war dog can't be fat. It has to be fit, for its own safety as well as its handler's. But while they'd been in Washington, Toushi Harada had given Ben a packet of fish rice crackers, which were Caesar's absolute favourite treat in the whole world. Reaching into a pouch on his belt, Ben took out one of the Japanese crackers and held it out to his EDD. Caesar gently took the biscuit and downed it in an instant.

Meanwhile, Charlie was at the lectern, practising his speech. It was about the work of GRRR; in particular, the unit's rescue of the Secretary-General of the United Nations after he had been taken hostage in Afghanistan by Taliban insurgents.

Once Charlie had finished running through his presentation, he sighed. 'I don't like giving speeches,' he said into the microphone, looking at the manager.

'It's part of the job, mate,' said Ben. 'You're GRRR's field commander, so people want to hear from you about our field ops.'

'I'd rather be in the field on one of those ops,' Charlie remarked, folding his speech and putting it in his tunic pocket. 'Give me action instead of speeches any day.'

CHAPTER 5

Wearing a shaggy black wig, baseball cap and sunglasses, and perspiring with nervousness, Manny Diaz strode into busy Big Sam's Restaurant and Bakery on East Houston Street. He found an empty table by the window, looking out to the street and the Texas National Bank on the corner opposite. The street was lined with parked cars, but one in particular caught Manny's eye – a grey GMC Savana van parked directly outside the bank. He smiled approvingly to himself.

When a young waitress came to him, Manny ordered a regular coffee and a doughnut. He checked whether his watch was working, then double-checked the time on the clock above the restaurant's servery. He took out his phone and, after confirming that it was indeed on, placed it on the table in front of him.

He could hear a man and a woman arguing behind him. After a time, the man turned around in his seat. 'What do you think, buddy?' he asked Manny.

'Think about what?' Manny responded distractedly.

He shifted slightly to face the couple but kept an eye on the entrance to the bank.

'My girlfriend says she's an *actor*, but I say she's an *actress*,' replied the balding man. 'A girl is an actress, right? Back me up here.'

At this moment the waitress arrived with a coffeepot, cup and saucer, and a doughnut on a plate, for Manny.

'You're a waitress, right? Not a waiter?' Manny asked her, thinking this would settle the matter.

'I'm not a waiter, that's true,' said the young woman as she set cup and plate in front of Manny, then poured his coffee. 'Here at Big Sam's I think of myself more as a customer-service facilitator.'

This only made the couple laugh and continue their dispute, but it got Manny off the hook. Turning his back to them, he took a sip and a bite, then reached into his pocket and pulled out two small slips of paper. Manny had read and re-read the numbers printed on them until one in the morning, when he was certain he knew them off by heart. But just to be on the safe side, he'd brought the pieces of paper along. If he had a sudden lapse of memory, he'd told himself, he could refer to them. Lopez had warned him he was a dead man if he screwed up this job. Whatever happened, Manny was determined that Rocky Marron would die today, just as Antonio Lopez planned.

Manny checked his watch: 11.10 am. In fifty minutes' time, Rocky Marron was due to arrive to make a deposit.

It would take Rocky at least half a dozen paces to cross the broad pavement to the bank door. All Manny had to do was call one of the numbers. After a single ring, an electrical pulse from the phone would detonate the bomb. What could possibly go wrong?

🐾🐾

Four blocks away, at the Sheraton Gunter Hotel, Charlie Grover was two-thirds of the way through his speech in front of a packed audience. Senior policemen from across the United States, Canada and Mexico had travelled to San Antonio to hear about the hostage-rescue work of the otherwise highly top-secret UN Global Rapid Reaction Responders. To protect his anonymity, Charlie was identified simply as Sergeant G. Delegates were also barred from taking his photograph.

With five minutes to go, Charlie introduced Ben and Caesar to the audience, adding, 'For security reasons, my GRRR colleague Sergeant F cannot be identified or photographed. But, because of the international fame of his explosive detection dog, you are free to identify Caesar.'

As Ben led Caesar to the dais, the applause was thunderous.

'Caesar is a highly trained and very experienced explosive detection dog, or EDD,' Charlie continued.

'A professor of English tells me that the title "explosive detection dog" is technically incorrect, because it literally means a detection dog which explodes.'

This brought hoots of laughter from the audience.

'Let me assure you, ladies and gentlemen,' Charlie went on, 'Caesar does not explode.' He waited for the laughter to die down before he continued. 'Caesar can detect even a hint of explosives with his ultra-sensitive nose. In the SAS he's known as "the super-sniffer". But, unlike a drug detection dog, a prison sniffer dog or a quarantine inspection dog, Caesar is put in harm's way every time he and his handler go out on a job. A number of EDDs have been killed or injured while on operations. Dogs like Caesar operate in open country and indoors with equal skill. Increasingly, in urban environments, terrorists and criminals are using improvised explosive devices. Sometimes those IEDs are sophisticated, sometimes they are basic, like fertiliser bombs. Caesar can detect them all.'

Caesar looked up at Ben each time Charlie mentioned his name, half-expecting a call to action. There was a look on his face that seemed to say, *What's happening, boss?*

'He can even identify individuals who have been handling explosives or have come in contact with explosives up to twenty-four hours earlier – as Caesar and Sergeant F are about to demonstrate. Prior to entering this room, several of you were chosen at random and given an envelope, with the request that you hold onto the envelope until the end of this session. One of those envelopes contains explosives residue.'

A murmur rippled through the audience as delegates looked around to see who was holding the envelopes in question.

Ben unclipped Caesar's leash. Pointing to the right side of the room, he commanded, 'Caesar, seek on!'

Caesar immediately rose up and, with his nose down, trotted along the front row, then down the side of the room, as all eyes in the audience followed him. Caesar came around the back of the room then down the central aisle. Halfway down the aisle, he stopped. Looking intently at a female superintendent from the Royal Canadian Mounted Police sitting beside the aisle, Caesar eased his rear end to the carpeted floor and stared at her.

'Ma'am, do you have an envelope for me?' Charlie asked.

Nodding, the woman held it up.

'A security officer is now going to test that envelope,' Charlie announced.

Sure enough, the chief security guard who had patted Charlie down earlier was standing at the back of the room. Carrying a portable electronic explosive detector the size of a mini vacuum cleaner, he came and took the envelope from the woman. With the whole room watching, the security guard swiped the envelope with the detector. There was a piercing electronic squawk.

'Traces of explosive chemicals, Sergeant,' announced the security guard.

'Traces of explosive chemicals,' Charlie repeated, and the room burst into applause.

Ben now gave Caesar the 'Return quickly' whistle. Caesar immediately jumped up. He trotted down the aisle to Ben and sat by his right side, looking at the audience.

'Good job, mate,' said Ben, patting Caesar, as appreciative applause continued from the audience.

'So, you see, ladies and gentlemen,' said Charlie, 'an EDD is an indispensable part of the GRRR team. Now, I know that many police services employ police dogs and that some of those dogs are trained as EDDs. But certain breeds, such as German shepherds, are not suitable for the type of work that Caesar is called upon to do. Often, too, EDDs are brought in as a last resort. Our experience is that an EDD should be part of the team from day one and involved in the primary deployment of first responders at any scene where there is the possibility that explosives are present.'

'And that covers a wide range of scenarios,' Ben added.

'That's right,' said Charlie. 'Caesar has been inserted by helicopter and by parachute, both HALO and LALO.

He has even been inserted by mini-submarine. We can use Caesar for solo forward reconnaissance, and for this we equip him with a video camera and transmitter. We also use Caesar for old-fashioned sniff-and-find tracking of hostages and suspects. He has saved many lives. Caesar, possessing skills that we humans do not, gives us the edge over the bad guys.'

At this point Caesar snorted, as if to agree.

Charlie glanced fondly at the labrador. 'And he's as much a part of our GRRR family as any human.'

In Big Sam's Restaurant and Bakery, Manny pushed his empty coffee cup toward the waitress.

'You want something else to eat?' the waitress asked, refilling his cup. She picked up his empty plate with her free hand.

Manny looked at his watch: 11.55. 'No, just the check,' he replied.

'Check coming right up,' said the waitress, walking off to collect his bill from the register.

Manny looked out the window, his heart beating fast with just five minutes to go before '*boom*' time. The late-morning traffic was thick outside, and he wondered if Rocky might be delayed. He pulled his phone closer, reciting two numbers to himself.

In the lobby of the Sheraton Gunter Hotel, Charlie and Ben were deep in conversation with Captain De Silva and Sergeant Austin when the red-uniformed Superintendent Brenda Michaels came striding up to them. This was the same Canadian superintendent who had held the envelope containing explosive chemical residue. She was a diminutive woman, little more than five feet tall, with short grey hair and sparkling green eyes.

'Thank you for cooperating with our demonstration, ma'am,' said Ben, recognising her.

A smile appeared on Superintendent Michaels' face. 'My pleasure,' she responded. 'You guys carried out a very effective demonstration. Of course, the Mounties have been using police dogs and EDDs for a long time. In fact, we had police dog teams before we began recruiting female officers for regular police duties back in 1974.'

'The Mounties hired dogs before they hired women?' Captain De Silva said with surprise.

'It was a pretty male-dominated, misogynistic world back in the seventies.' Michaels shrugged. 'But, hey, you guys here in San Antonio have one of the lowest percentages of female to male officers in the United States – just seven per cent of your officers are female, if I remember correctly.'

De Silva looked embarrassed. 'Yeah, well . . .'

Michaels turned to Charlie. 'Sergeant, in your speech you mentioned that German shepherds don't make good EDDs. The RCMP uses German shepherds exclusively, so I was wondering who is right – you or us?'

'Sergeant F can best answer that, Superintendent,' Charlie replied, turning to his friend.

Ben nodded. 'Caesar has a bit of German shepherd in him, Superintendent,' he said. 'Maybe that gives him his steely courage – he's afraid of nothing. But a purebred German shepherd can be a "one master dog". He can snap and snarl at those around him to "protect" his master, which is no good when an EDD like Caesar has to spend hours, days and sometimes weeks in the field with a team of soldiers. I couldn't have Caesar snapping and snarling at Sergeant G, for example, when we're on an op.'

'I take your point,' Superintendent Michaels conceded, 'but a labrador like this lovely guy here doesn't have the same power to daunt criminals that a German shepherd has.'

'A snarling, barking German shepherd is a pretty daunting sight,' Ben agreed. 'That's great when you want a guard dog that warns you of intruders, or if you want to intimidate felons.'

'Particularly armed felons.'

'Sure, but silence is one of the key weapons of a special ops team. We often can't speak for hours at a time, communicating only by hand signals.'

'How then do you issue commands to Caesar in that kind of situation?' asked Michaels.

'The same as everyone else – by hand signal,' Ben replied.

'Caesar recognises up to two hundred hand signals,' Charlie added proudly.

'Two hundred?' Michaels echoed, astonished. 'You're kidding me!'

Charlie smiled. 'I taught him some of them myself, when Caesar was my care dog for a while.'

'Want a demo?' Ben asked.

'A demo?'

'A demonstration,' said Ben.

'Ah. Sure.'

'Got an ATM card on you?' When the superintendent nodded, Ben said, 'Can you take it out and hold it by one end, please?'

Superintendent Michaels took out her Visa card. Ben eased down onto one knee in front of the seated Caesar, unclipped his leash and, with a hand signal involving both hands, silently gave him instructions. Then he pointed to the card in the superintendent's hand and then across the lobby to an ATM. Caesar trotted over to the Canadian superintendent and carefully took the credit card from her fingers. Card in mouth, he then turned and made his way across the lobby. He was a dog on a mission.

Ben, Charlie, Superintendent Michaels, Captain De Silva and Sergeant Austin all followed the brown labrador. Hotel guests turned with looks of wonder on their faces to watch the dog pass. A pair of young newlyweds stepped aside to allow Caesar access to the ATM. Standing up on his hind legs, he put his front paws on the machine and pushed the superintendent's card into the appropriate slot. The ATM accepted the card, swallowing it with an electronic hum.

'I wouldn't have believed it if I hadn't seen it with my own eyes,' said Michaels.

Ben grinned and patted Caesar before he reattached the leash to his collar. 'Caesar can't punch in your PIN for you. But you're not supposed to tell anyone your PIN, right?' Ben added with a wink.

🐾🐾

Manny Diaz saw a black Chrysler 300C draw to a halt beside the van accross the street. He glanced at his watch: 12.00. Tall, athletic, curly headed Rocky Marron emerged from a rear door of the sedan and looked warily up and down the street. He was on time – dead on time. Manny held his phone in his hand, his index finger poised over the keypad. But his mind had gone blank.

He couldn't remember the number he was supposed to dial to set off the bomb. In fact, he couldn't remember either of the numbers he had to dial. Trying not to panic, he reached into his pocket. With a shaky hand, he took out the two pieces of paper.

'Thank God!' he gasped to himself. If he had disposed of these slips of paper as Antonio Lopez had instructed him, he would be lost right now.

The waitress placed the bill in front of him. 'Your check, sir.'

'*Sí, sí*,' he said absently, staring at the two pieces of paper. 'But which number is the first one?'

'Excuse me?' said the waitress.

'Which number? Which number is first?' Manny mumbled, looking out the window.

Rocky was on the move. Carrying a small suitcase, he had stepped up onto the pavement.

'God help me,' whispered Manny. He hastily chose a number, hoping and praying it was the right one. As he dialled the number, Rocky Marron began walking toward the entrance to the bank. Manny put the phone to his ear. He heard it ring once.

CHAPTER 6

In the lobby of the Sheraton Gunter, everyone heard a distant *boom*, followed immediately by the sound of shattering glass.

Ben had heard enough bombs go off over the years to recognise the sound. 'Bomb!' he declared.

Simultaneously, Caesar's head came up and turned in the direction of the noise. After all the ops he'd been through with Ben, he also knew a bomb blast when he heard one.

'Let's go!' yelled Captain De Silva. He led a dash to the hotel's front door by all the members of the group who had only moments before been marvelling at Caesar's extraordinary abilities. Superintendent Michaels was one of them.

Once the group was outside, they could see a pall of smoke rising above East Houston Street. Car and building alarms blared in a tuneless, high-pitched cacophony.

'It went off in the street, not in a building,' De Silva surmised from the location of the rising smoke. 'So it's unlikely to be a gas explosion.'

Ben looked over at Charlie. 'It was a bomb, right?'

'Roger to that, mate,' said Charlie. 'Let's take a look.'

'We might be able to help out on the scene,' said De Silva.

'I'm coming, too,' said Michaels, as all six of them set off in the direction of the explosion. 'I'm proficient in first aid.'

Terrified pedestrians flooded by them, running in the opposite direction to get away from the explosion as fast as they could.

'Be careful,' Ben cautioned the group, with Caesar loping along at his side. 'IEDs often come in pairs – in Afghanistan, in the Middle East, at the 2013 Boston Marathon. One bomb to suck in the first responders, then a second bomb to cut them down.'

They crossed several intersections. Police sirens were wailing in the distance. Traffic in East Houston and intersecting streets had come to a halt. Several San Antonio policemen who had been on foot patrol in the vicinity were also running toward the explosion. Ahead, a parked Toyota minibus was burning, its flames spreading to surrounding vehicles. Bloodied people lay near the wreckage, with passers-by bending over them, trying to help.

De Silva gasped. 'It's like a war zone!'

A jagged section of the rear of the minibus lay on the pavement in their path, with the words 'Texian Transit Company' visible on the scorched metal. Ben walked over to examine it. Bending down, he recognised the back cover piece of a popular brand of mobile phone lying beside it. 'Looks like it was detonated by mobile,' he called to Charlie.

Charlie nodded. 'We got ourselves a bomber here, mate.'

'Is there a time-delayed follow-up bomb?' Ben pondered aloud.

Charlie looked at his friend. 'If so, where?'

'Nearby,' Ben replied grimly. He stood up and surveyed the mayhem around them, thinking about where he would have hidden a second bomb if he were the bomber. 'In another car.'

🐾🐾

Manny gaped at the sight of Rocky Marron standing, alive and unharmed, on the pavement outside the Texas National Bank. Manny had chosen the wrong number and had set off the bomb in the Toyota minibus instead of the one in the GMC Savana van. He watched as Rocky ran back to the sedan. Desperately, Manny dialled the number on the other piece of paper, to set off the bomb in the van beside Rocky's Chrysler.

The phone rang once, twice, three times. But the bomb in the grey van across the street did not go off. Panicking, Manny looked at the phone's screen and realised he'd dialled a wrong number.

'Hello?' answered the owner of the wrong number.

Cursing, Manny terminated the call. He looked up to see Rocky sliding into the back of the Chrysler and pulling the door closed. Frantically, Manny dialled again. With smoking tyres and a roar from its powerful V8 engine, Rocky Marron's car sped off. Perspiring heavily, Manny held the phone to his ear. He listened as it connected and rang . . . and rang. Manny realised with horror that he'd dialled a wrong number *again*.

With the street to the east blocked by the wreckage of the first bomb, the Chrysler made a sharp turn and pushed into the traffic heading west, knocking aside vehicles as if they were toys. The Chrysler's route was going to bring it right past Big Sam's. Realising this, Manny cast aside his phone and rose to his feet. The phone slid across the table and clattered to the floor.

Everyone else in the restaurant was crowded around the windows trying to see what was going on. Manny brushed past the man who had tried to involve him in the dispute with his girlfriend, sending coffee from the cup in his hand spilling onto the table.

'Hey!' protested the customer.

Manny ignored him, but the young waitress stood in his way. She gestured to the unpaid bill sitting on his table. 'What about the check?'

Manny reached behind and grabbed a Glock 17 semi-automatic pistol from his belt. The handgun most widely used by law enforcement agencies around the world, made from plastic and steel, the Glock was sleek and black and lethal.

The sight of the pistol sent the waitress reeling back, out of his way. 'Don't shoot me!' she cried, fear written all over her face. 'Don't shoot me!'

Manny had no plans to shoot the waitress. His entire focus was on killing Rocky Marron. He knocked aside an elderly man as he came barrelling out of the restaurant and onto the pavement. At this moment the Chrysler 300C was passing Big Sam's. Manny lifted the pistol to the firing position, grasping his right wrist with his left hand to steady it, as he'd been trained to do in the army. Without pausing, Manny opened fire on the Chrysler. His first two rounds were aimed at the driver's door and window, the next two at the rear passenger compartment. *Blam-blam! Blam-blam!*

Bystanders screamed at the sound of the gunshots and flung themselves away. Determined to complete the job, Manny followed the Chrysler with his pistol raised. He knew that if he did not finish Rocky Marron, Antonio Lopez would finish Manny Diaz. It looked as if the Chrysler was going to escape, and Manny cursed aloud as he ran. At high speed, the Chrysler attempted to turn right into Broadway. Clipping the end of a yellow school bus, the Chrysler flipped up onto its side and, with a screech of metal and with sparks flying, went sliding across the intersection until it slammed into a taxi.

Dodging around vehicles, Manny raced to the Chrysler and fired through the rear window, spewing rounds into the car's rear compartment. Glass shattered and bullets whined off metal. Manny didn't stop until he was out of bullets, emptying the seventeen-round magazine into the back of the Chrysler. People on the sidewalk ducked for cover. Others stood open-mouthed, unable to believe that this was really happening.

'Put the gun down!' came a voice from behind.

Manny swung to see a bicycle patrolman standing twenty metres away. The man had a Smith & Wesson M&P40 pistol pointed at him with both hands. Manny didn't recognise the policeman, but this was one of the two bike cops that he and Lopez had observed from the roof the previous day.

'No way!' Manny responded, springing forward and setting off to run past the Chrysler and make his escape.

'Stop, or I'll fire!' bellowed the cop.

Manny kept running. The policeman didn't warn him again. He let off three shots in swift succession.

Blam-blam-blam! Manny fell headlong in the street, in front of dozens of shocked civilians. His empty Glock flew from his grip and went skidding across the street, coming to rest in a gutter. Manny lay where he had fallen, face down, unmoving, amid the traffic.

CHAPTER 7

Ben, Caesar and Charlie proved fitter and faster than their American and Canadian police colleagues. Twenty paces ahead of the other three, they reached the spot outside the Texas National Bank where Rocky Marron had been standing just minutes before. They knew nothing about Rocky or the plot to kill him. All they knew was that serveral gunshots had been fired. As they ran by the grey GMC Savana, intent on reaching the scene of the shooting just around the corner on Broadway, Caesar suddenly reared up and tried to dive toward the van.

'What's up with Caesar?' asked Charlie, stopping in his tracks. 'The action's all around the corner.'

'I don't know,' said Ben, allowing Caesar to lead him toward the parked van. 'Something's attracted him.'

Caesar eased his rear end onto the pavement beside the van. And there he sat, looking intently at the vehicle.

'What's got into your dog, Sergeant Fulton?' Captain De Silva panted as he reached them.

'That's his signature, Captain,' said Ben.

'His what?'

'His EDD signature. He's telling us that there's another bomb in this van.'

'What?'

'Clear the area,' said Ben. 'It must be big to attract Caesar's attention from a couple of metres away – and it could blow anytime.'

As Sergeant Austin and Superintendent Michaels caught up to the others, De Silva took out his phone.

'Don't use your phone!' Ben warned. 'You might set off the bomb. The first device was almost certainly detonated by a call from a mobile.'

De Silva put away his phone. 'Get everyone off the street!' he yelled to Austin and Michaels. 'Now!'

As the three senior police officers began to herd pedestrians back, Ben made a decision. 'I'm going to try to disarm the bomb,' he called to Charlie. 'If I'm right about it being triggered by a phone call, I could separate the phone from the explosives and disarm it. There's not enough time to wait for the bomb squad. It could go off any second. In which case, it'll take a lot of people along with it.'

Charlie nodded. Apart from all the pedestrians streaming from the scene, there were scores of people in vehicles who would be caught by the blast. 'Go ahead, but I'm staying with you.'

'Okay, you look underneath. I'll check the interior.'

'It could be booby-trapped.'

Ben met Charlie's gaze. 'I guess I'll have to take that risk.'

Several blocks away, sitting in the back of a yellow taxi with El Globo the bomb-maker, Antonio Lopez was not happy. He had heard an explosion – a *single* explosion. With the window down, Lopez waited for the sound of a second bomb. It never came.

'That imbecile Manny has screwed up!' Lopez raged. He turned to El Globo. 'Give me the numbers.'

'*Sí, Patrón.*' The bomb-maker, who had consigned the numbers to memory, began to reel them off.

'No, no, no! Write them for me! *Rápido!*'

El Globo hastily wrote down the two numbers, then handed his boss the piece of paper. Lopez immediately dialled the second number, assuming it was the second bomb that had failed to detonate, and put the phone to his ear.

With Caesar watching him intently, Ben opened the rear door to the van. Seeing nothing on the front or back seats, he stooped to look on the floor beneath them.

'There's something here!' he called as he spotted a package the size of several house bricks sitting side by side. It was wrapped in black plastic and positioned beneath the nearest of the rear seats.

'What is it?' asked Captain De Silva.

Ben looked around in surprise. 'What are you doing here, sir?'

'The others are clearing away the public. What do you need?'

Ben returned his attention to the package. 'I need a knife. There's a package taped to the leg of one of the seats. I'll have to cut it free.'

Normally, on active duty, Ben and Charlie would both be wearing equipment belts, and on each of their belts would be a Fairbairn–Sykes fighting knife. But, for their appearance at the Texas conference, both had come wearing only field uniform. Their arms and equipment had been left back at base in Australia. Captain De Silva was also wearing a uniform and was likewise supposed to be unarmed.

'Here.' Unbuttoning his jacket, De Silva withdrew a knife which he always wore on a scabbard beneath his jacket. The captain received a lot of death threats in his line of work and, for self-protection, he never went anywhere unarmed. He held the knife out to Ben. 'Be my guest, partner.'

'Thanks.' Taking the knife, Ben carefully sliced through the duct tape that secured the package to the metal leg of the seat. He was then able to slide the package out onto clear floor space. Caesar, sitting on the pavement behind him, whined.

'I know, I know, Caesar,' said Ben as he quickly studied the package. 'You can smell the explosives in here, can't you?' He sensed De Silva looking over his right shoulder and Charlie looking over his left. 'You two blokes should be taking cover. No use all of us going up in smoke if I make a mistake.'

'I'm not going anywhere, mate,' Charlie said firmly.

'That goes for me too,' said Captain De Silva.

'Okay. There's no time to argue about it.' Ben could see that the otherwise flat-sided parcel had a bulge on the top corresponding with the shape and size of a mobile phone. Using the knife, Ben carefully slit the black plastic around the mound. Sure enough, he revealed a mobile phone. Its screen glowed with life. Beneath the phone, Ben could see detonators jammed into yellow sticks of plastic explosive – enough to demolish half the block. A thin red electrical wire trailed from the phone to the detonators. 'My gut feeling is to cut the wire leading from the phone,' he said.

'It could have a sophisticated booby-trap built in, Ben,' Charlie warned. 'One that sets the whole thing off if you cut the wire.'

Ben nodded. He and Charlie had come across just that kind of booby-trap before. But, Ben reasoned to himself, those had been bombs created by professional military armourers. And those bombs were generally planted with the intention of being discovered, so that the booby-trap was triggered, killing the bomb-disposal expert trying to disarm it. He told himself that this bomb had more likely been created by an amateur, a civilian without the knowledge or skill to include a booby-trap. And as the first bomb had been detonated, this one was probably intended for remote detonation as well – and at any moment. Removing his blue beret, Ben mopped his brow.

'To cut, or not to cut, that is the question,' he said, lifting the red wire with his left hand and raising the knife with his right.

🐾🐾

Lopez cursed as the number he'd dialled was put through to voicemail. He glared at El Globo beside him. 'These numbers *are* correct?'

The bomb-maker nodded vigorously. '*Sí, Patrón*. Try the other one.'

'This had better work, *amigo*,' growled Lopez. 'It had better set off the other bomb. Call the numbers out to me, one at a time.'

Lopez punched in the number of the phone that sat atop the black plastic package on the floor of the van on East Houston Street – the phone with the red wire connected to the detonator. The wire that was now in Ben Fulton's hand. Satisfied that he had entered the right sequence of numbers, Lopez moved his index finger to the green button.

'Now for bang number two!' he said, stabbing 'call' with his finger.

Caesar, aware of the need for swift action, barked urgently at Ben.

'Yes, mate. Here goes,' said Ben. Taking a deep breath, he sliced the wire connecting the phone to the bomb.

A fraction of a second after the sharp blade cleaved the wire in two, the phone rang. All eyes turned to the bomb. The phone continued to ring but nothing happened. Ben had successfully disarmed the bomb – just in the nick of time. Had he waited another second before cutting the wire, Antonio Lopez's call would have come through and, after just one ring, they would all have been blown sky-high.

As the phone continued to ring, Ben took it up and answered it. 'Sorry, mate, your bomb won't be going off today,' he said into the phone. The phone went dead in his ear. He looked at Charlie, and grinned. 'Someone isn't very happy with us.'

'Give me that phone,' said Captain De Silva. 'My guys will be able to identify the caller's number.'

Antonio Lopez cursed and tossed his phone out of the taxi's open window in disgust.

'What now, *Patrón*?' asked the driver.

'Let's go,' Lopez instructed sourly. 'Don't break any speed limits.'

The taxi edged out into slow-moving traffic.

'Who answered the call, *Patrón*?' asked El Globo.

'Some *gringo*, but not a Yankee. He called me "mate".'

El Globo frowned. 'How did the *gringo* get hold of the phone attached to the bomb?'

'That is a good question, *amigo*,' Lopez responded thoughtfully.

'Bomb squad?'

'Whoever he is, he will pay for interfering in my business,' said Lopez. 'Pay with his life!'

CHAPTER 8

In the most expensive house in one of the poorest neighbourhoods in the city of Monterrey, Mexico, behind high concrete walls topped with barbed wire, a man lay on a black leather sofa, watching television and eating fried chicken. Six huge LCD screens were lined up in a row in front of him. One streamed internet data while the others were tuned to different channels. The audio from each competed with the others, creating a discordant mishmash of sound. The full-length drapes on the windows were all drawn, cloaking the room in darkness, with the only light in the room coming from the flickering screens.

The man was aged in his forties, with his thick, black hair slicked back like Elvis Presley. He prided himself on looking a lot like Elvis, and needed little encouragement to croon one of the singer's famous ballads. He wore loose white trousers, a white singlet and a green jungle-print silk shirt that was open to his waist. He was Carlos Marron, alias El Loro Verde – the Green Parrot.

'San Antonio?' he suddenly said with surprise. Sitting up, he lay aside the drumstick he'd been eating. He reached for the remote control and turned up the volume, listening with growing concern to a news report about an incident that had just taken place across the border.

'San Antonio police say that a bomb exploded at high noon in an empty bus in San Antonio's financial district, not far from the famous Alamo battle site,' said a female television reporter. She was standing in East Houston Street, police and emergency workers milling around the wreckage behind her.

'God in heaven!' exclaimed Marron, recognising the location as the place where his brother, Rocky, made his deposits. He turned up the volume even more.

'Seventeen people injured at the scene have been taken to hospitals in the downtown area. Meanwhile, at least two males are dead. Police have yet to confirm the identities of any of the victims, but the incident is believed to be gang-related and sources close to the SAPD have told Channel Five News that one of the deceased is Mexican crime cartel figure Eduardo "Rocky" Marron.'

'What! My little brother, dead?' The blood drained from Marron's face. 'Vargas! Vargas! Get in here, now!'

Enrico Vargas, a flabby man with an ugly scar that ran from his left cheek and down his neck came bustling into the room. 'What is it, *Padrino*?'

'Get Rocky on the phone.' Marron jabbed a finger toward one of the television screens. 'They say he is dead. There has been a bomb.'

'A bomb, *Padrino*?'

'*Sí!* Call Rocky now! He cannot be dead.'

Vargas took out his phone to call Rocky. Meanwhile, El Loro, now sitting on the edge of his seat, returned his attention to the news report.

'. . . and the SAPD has revealed that one of the deceased bears the star tattoo of the Estrella crime cartel,' said the reporter. 'Both Rocky Marron and his injured driver were known to be members of the rival Árbol cartel. This has all the hallmarks of a cartel turf war, right here in downtown San Antonio. It appears the Estrella cartel were out to get Rocky Marron, brother of the head of the Árbol cartel, Carlos Marron, or as he is more commonly known, El Loro Verde – the Green Parrot.'

'Rocky is not answering his phone, *Padrino*,' said Vargas. 'It just goes straight to voicemail.'

'Keep trying,' Marron snapped, his eyes glued to the television.

'Captain Leo De Silva of the SAPD says the collateral damage could have been much higher here today,' continued the reporter, 'had it not been for the presence of Caesar, the famous Australian explosive detection dog.'

The news report cut to an earlier interview between the reporter and Captain De Silva. 'Yes, we were real lucky that Caesar and his handler were at a conference nearby. Caesar located a second bomb, just outside the Texas National Bank.'

'Captain, do you think the Estrella cartel is out to eliminate the Árbol cartel's leaders?' asked the reporter.

'It sure looks that way,' said Captain De Silva. 'If I were the Green Parrot, I would be looking over my shoulder. I think this signals that Estrella is out to get him.'

'So,' said the reporter, 'we owe a vote of thanks to the famous Caesar, and his handler, whose identity we can't reveal for security reasons.' The picture briefly cut to Caesar being led along the pavement by Ben, whose face was blurred. 'I am told that Caesar is the finest, most decorated explosive detection dog in the world. But even Caesar's presence could not save Rocky Marron. You have to wonder if he would still be alive if Caesar had been on the scene a little earlier.'

'Still no answer from Rocky, *Padrino*,' said Vargas. 'Could it really be that he is dead?'

'My brother, dead.' Marron dropped his head in despair. When he looked up, there was a fierce determination in his eyes. 'Get me that dog!' he commanded, pointing at the television screen.

'*Padrino?*'

'Get me that dog! Get this César for me. Those Estrella cowards will not kill *me* with their bombs. Get me the best bomb-detecting dog in the world.

This dog.' Coming to his feet, he stabbed a finger at the television.

'But . . . how, *Padrino*?' Vargas stammered.

'How do I know? Just do it, Vargas! Whatever it takes. You get this César for me. This dog will be my protector and the protector of my family.'

'But kidnap a dog . . .?'

'*Sí!* How hard can it be to kidnap a dog? Do it, Vargas. Get this César for me!'

🐾🐾

Ben and Charlie had intended to catch a ride with a USAF transport plane that evening, to an air base in California. From there they would fly back to Australia. Meanwhile, Caesar was required by Australian law to spend time in a quarantine facility. Ben had found a suitable facility in San Antonio, one that met the high standards set by Australian animal health regulations. It was run by Joe Levine, a former US military dog handler. Caesar would spend a 'holiday' at Joe's Doghouse while he waited out the quarantine period prior to returning to Australia. But first Ben and Charlie had delayed their own return to Australia to attend a meeting, at the invitation of the SAPD.

Captain De Silva had immediately created a joint task force with officers from the SAPD and the Texas

Rangers, involving investigators, forensic experts, computer whizzes and specialists in the criminal activities of Mexican cartels. The day following the bombing, the Australian visitors sat in on the briefing that De Silva gave to the fifty Texas police officers assigned to the task force. Grim-faced, the participants sat around a conference room at SAPD headquarters as the captain brought everyone up to date.

Special guests Ben, Caesar and Charlie were directed to the front row. Caesar was the centre of attention, with half the police officers they passed wanting to give him a friendly pat. Once Ben and Charlie took their seats, Caesar lay at Ben's feet, seemingly disinterested. But every now and then his ears would prick up.

'So, three dead and seventeen in hospital,' Captain De Silva began, standing at the front of the packed room. A large LED screen sat on the wall behind him. 'The Mexican cartels think they can bring their civil war to the streets of San Antonio, do they?' he said, barely controlling the anger in his voice. 'I don't think so! Let me tell you, these guys have got another thing coming if they think we're gonna let Texas become another cartel battleground. That's why our ancestors fought and died at the Alamo – to free this state of rule by the gun!'

'You got that right, Leo!' declared Captain Ed Franco from the Texas Rangers. 'We gotta find the people responsible for this outrage and put them before a judge and jury! We gotta send a signal to the criminals and to the good people of Texas – there ain't no place for mob-style law in this great state. I got that direct from the State Governor himself.'

'You won't hear any arguments from anyone in this room, Ed,' De Silva agreed. 'Fortunately, we had Sergeant F and Caesar on hand yesterday. If it hadn't been for them, the second IED would have detonated, killing and maiming a heap more people.'

At the mention of his name, Caesar raised his head. He looked left and right with a look that seemed to say, *Someone want to play?*

'Sergeant F disarmed the bomb with just seconds to spare,' continued De Silva. 'Would you believe the phone that was supposed to set off the second IED rang while Ben was holding it? We were all *this* close to being toast.' He held up a finger and thumb to indicate a distance of just a few centimetres. Then he took up a remote control. 'So, here's what we know so far.'

He clicked and the screen behind him came to life. The police mug shots of three men appeared on the screen, side by side.

'These are yesterday's victims.' He pointed to the screen. 'Eduardo "Rocky" Marron, younger brother of the head of the Árbol cartel, Carlos Marron. Rocky was a senior *capitán* in his brother's cartel – died from gunshot wounds received from a single assailant. Second, Alberto Estevez, Rocky's driver and a low-level Árbol member, who died in hospital overnight from multiple gunshot wounds inflicted by the same assailant. And finally, the assailant, Manny Diaz, a mid-level member of the rival Estrella cartel, shot dead at the scene by a uniformed SAPD officer after ignoring a challenge and trying to escape on foot.'

'You think Manny set off the bomb and shot the other two?' said Charlie.

De Silva nodded. 'Affirmative, Sergeant G. We know that Manny shot both Rocky and Estevez following the detonation of the first IED, before he was shot and killed by Officer Pete O'May. From witnesses in Big Sam's, it's pretty clear that Manny set off the first IED with his phone, but for some reason was unable to set off the second. Manny was dead in the street by the time Sergeant F took the call on the phone connected to the second IED. Meaning, that call was placed by someone *other* than Manny. Any questions?'

'Why did Manny kill the other two, sir?' Ben asked. 'What was his motive? And why here, in San Antonio?'

'We found a pile of cash in a suitcase in the hotted-up Chrysler that Rocky and Estevez were using. And we know from witnesses that Rocky was heading into the Texas National Bank on the corner of East Houston and Broadway when the IED exploded.'

'Was Manny after the money?' Ben asked.

De Silva clicked the remote and a photograph of the bank's exterior appeared on the screen.

'I think it was a hit, pure and simple. Rocky was trying to make a getaway when Manny unloaded his Glock into the car.' The picture was replaced with an image of the bullet-riddled Chrysler lying on its side. 'We've also now established that Rocky made a regular cash deposit at this branch, into an account in the name of Alamo City Cleaners, a legitimate laundry and dry-cleaning business based on San Antonio's south side. We think that Alamo City Cleaners is a front for the Árbol cartel in Texas.'

'A money-laundering laundry,' quipped Tex Austin, generating laughs around the room. 'They put the proceeds of crime through its books.'

'Captain,' said Charlie, 'could you fill Sergeant F and myself in on the Árbol and Estrella cartels and their leaders?'

'Sure thing, Sergeant,' De Silva responded. 'Árbol is Spanish for "tree". The Árbol cartel has been around for more than forty years, and its name reflects the fact that it has branches above ground while its roots spread unseen everywhere underground. Seven or eight years ago, when competition between cartels was intensifying, Árbol recruited the Estrella boys from the Mexican Armed Forces to be their muscle. The Estrella boys acted as the bodyguards for Árbol leaders and kept their low-level operatives in line. If there was conflict with other cartels, it was Estrella *pistoleros*, or gunmen, who were on the firing line for Árbol.'

'But the Estrella blokes fell out with their Árbol masters?' said Charlie.

'Right on the money,' said De Silva. 'The Estrella boys decided they wanted more than the thousands of dollars they were being paid. They wanted the millions that Árbol was raking in every week from their criminal activities.'

'What kind of criminal activities?' Ben asked.

'Protection rackets, kidnapping and extortion, robberies, gambling, prostitution, gun-running, drug-running – you name it. Árbol also had a kind of code of honour, where they didn't get involved in anything that was harmful to kids. Estrella don't abide by that code.'

'Crooks with a code of honour are still crooks,' Charlie remarked.

'Árbol's code is like a smoker doing loads of exercise, thinking that will make up for the damage they're doing to their lungs,' De Silva agreed. 'Twisting logic to justify the harm they're doing.'

'And to justify the money they're making,' Ben added.

'Estrella don't care who gets hurt,' said De Silva. 'They're trained killers, with no scruples. And they wanted Árbol to get more heavily involved in narcotics, to make more money. When the Árbol leadership wouldn't agree, the Estrella group broke away and set up on their own.'

'Captain, where did the Estrella name come from?' Charlie asked.

'Estrella means "star". They consider themselves the stars of the Mexican crime world. After the split, in 2004, there was a brief and bitter war between the two cartels until the Green Parrot organised a truce with the chief of Estrella, Raphael Vicente. It's been an uneasy alliance but it has held up until now. Our sources tell us that Vicente has recently died from cancer, and this has left Antonio Lopez in charge of Estrella. Let me tell you, Lopez will stop at nothing to bring Árbol under his control. My theory is that he's the one behind Rocky Marron's assassination. I think that Lopez is out to destroy the Árbol leadership, to move in on Árbol's criminal territory.'

'So, you think the Green Parrot is next on his hit list?' Ben asked.

De Silva nodded. 'You got it.'

'You don't think that Estrella is just sending Árbol a message, Captain?' Tex Austin asked.

'It was a message, sure enough, and the message was "I'm coming to get you, Marron", said De Silva. 'It was easier to get the Green Parrot's brother here in the US. But Lopez will be looking for a way to get Carlos Marron in Mexico, don't you worry.'

'Tell us about the Green Parrot,' said Charlie.

'He's a fan of Elvis Presley,' De Silva said with a smile. 'Marron's been known to dress as Elvis and sing a few of his numbers to entertain his gang members. He is smart. In fact, he's cunning as a fox. That's how he's avoided jail all these years. It will be interesting to see how he reacts to the assassination of his little brother and to see what he does to protect himself. Will he go after Lopez? Will he launch a full-scale war against Estrella? If he does, that spells trouble for a whole bunch of people – ourselves included.'

CHAPTER 9

A few days later, Sergeant Austin drove Ben and Caesar to Joe's Doghouse, in the Far West Side of San Antonio, not far from Government Canyon State Natural Area. Ben sat in the back of the sergeant's station wagon for the drive out along a freeway. Caesar began the journey sitting beside Ben, but before long he lay down with his head on his master's lap. Every now and then he would lift his head and try to lick Ben's face. He could sense that they would soon be parting.

Staff were hosing down concrete-and-wire animal enclosures when the station wagon drove up the poplar-lined driveway to the quarantine facility, which spread over several acres. A sign said: 'Canines and their two-legged friends welcome at Joe's Doghouse.' Once the station wagon pulled up, Ben and Sergeant Austin alighted, and their ears were immediately met by barking and howling. Caesar heard this too and, dropping his head, lingered on the back seat.

'Come on, Caesar, out you get,' Ben said, clicking his fingers.

But Caesar didn't budge. He looked directly ahead, as if he hadn't seen or heard Ben's instruction.

'What's got into him?' Sergeant Austin asked with a frown. 'Or didn't he hear you?'

Ben smiled to himself. 'He heard me just fine. Caesar's heard all the barking and knows what's going to happen. I thought he was being especially affectionate on the drive here. He usually knows before the event that we're going to be separated for a while.'

'Doggy sixth sense?'

'Something like that.'

'And I guess that all these barking dogs here are telling him that the place is full of lonely mutts?'

'I'm afraid so. Imagine how we'd feel if we arrived at a hotel and all you could hear was the sound of unhappy occupants yelling and complaining. Can't be helped, though. We have to go through with this.' Ben clicked his fingers again. 'Out you get, Caesar,' he said, more firmly than before, pointing to the ground at his feet. 'Right here!'

This time Caesar complied, jumping down to the ground and taking a seat beside his master. He glanced up at Ben with a sad expression, as if to say, *Please don't leave me here, boss.*

Ben fixed his leash to the labrador's collar. 'Rules are rules, mate. There was a time when war dogs weren't allowed back into Australia at all after overseas service, so we're lucky we can get you back.'

While Sergeant Austin waited outside, Ben led Caesar in through the facility's glass front doors.

A khaki-uniformed receptionist, a girl of no more than eighteen, saw the pair and smiled.

'Hi there! Welcome to Joe's Doghouse,' she said in a chirpy voice. Her eyes dropped to Caesar, who trotted along beside Ben with both his head and tail low. 'And you must be Caesar. We were expecting you – all the way from Australia, I hear.' She raised her gaze to Ben. 'Does he only understand Australian, sir? Or will he be okay with our American attendants? No one here speaks Australian.'

Ben chuckled. 'We speak English in Australia. Caesar will understand everything your staff say to him as long as it's not in Spanish,' he replied. 'Even then, he'd pick up the gist of what was being said from the tone of the speaker's voice and their body language. Besides, Caesar knows a couple hundred hand signals, so spoken commands are not always necessary.'

The receptionist beamed. 'Wow! What a clever dog. I wish my dog would obey hand signals. That would be real cool.'

'It's all a matter of training,' Ben assured her.

As they were talking, a tall, bald man with a neat grey beard emerged from a glass-walled office behind the reception desk. Like the receptionist, he wore a khaki uniform emblazoned with the Joe's Doghouse logo.

'Howdy!' he said, advancing toward them with a welcoming smile. 'This wouldn't be the famous Caesar, by any chance?'

'Sure is.' Ben looked the man up and down. His skin resembled tanned leather – he was clearly an outdoorsman. Ben guessed the fellow was close to seventy years old, but he walked with the sprightliness of a man forty years younger.

'Joe Levine,' the man introduced himself, grasping Ben by the hand with a vice-like grip. He then squatted beside Caesar. 'Howdy, Caesar boy. Welcome to my doghouse.' He ruffled Caesar's neck.

Caesar immediately took a liking to the big American. His tail began to wag and he attempted to lick Joe on the cheek.

'He likes you,' said Ben.

'And I like him,' said Joe, giving Caesar a pat on the flank before coming back to his feet. 'His reputation precedes him. I'm sorry we don't have a presidential suite here for a dog as famous as Caesar. But we'll look after him, don't you worry, Sergeant.'

Despite the warm welcome from the facility's owner, Caesar now pressed against Ben's leg and looked up at him with a look that seemed to say, *Let me stay with you, boss.*

Ben felt a twinge of guilt. Dropping to one knee, he pulled the labrador into an embrace. 'It can't be helped, mate,' he said soothingly. 'Unless you want to stay in America for the rest of your days, we both have to go through this separation for a while.'

'I guess you've both been through this a few times before,' said Joe.

'We sure have,' Ben said sadly, straightening again.

'I had a lab like Caesar when I served in Vietnam,' said Joe. 'Had to leave him behind when we pulled out. Weren't no quarantine arrangements for war dogs back then.'

'That must have been tough.'

'It was tough. My dog, Star, went to a guy in the South Vietnamese Government. He had a big French colonial mansion in Saigon with loads of garden space for Star to run around in. But, of course, the North Vietnamese overran the south after the US pulled out, and the South Vietnamese Government fell.'

'What happened to your dog?'

'I heard that his new owner disappeared after becoming a prisoner of the North Vietnamese. I've been back to Vietnam twice but have never been able to find out what happened to him, or to Star. His colonial mansion in Saigon is a school now. And of course the name of Saigon was changed to Ho Chi Minh City. Everything had changed. And no one knew a darn thing about Star.'

'Sorry to hear that,' said Ben. 'I know how close a

military handler and his dog become. Caesar is part of my family, and we've been through a lot together.'

'You got that right, part of the family.' Joe sighed. 'Losing Star was like losing my kid.' Feeling the mood dip, he promptly made a conscious effort to shake off his melancholy. 'So, you can be sure that we're going to take real good care of Caesar. He'll be like part of our family.' He glanced over at the receptionist. 'Right, Cindy?'

'Right, Pops,' Cindy replied.

'Cindy's my granddaughter,' Joe explained proudly.

'Did you receive my email detailing Caesar's dietary requirements and exercise regime?' Ben asked. 'It's essential they be followed.'

Joe nodded. 'It's all in the system.' He held out a hand, to take Caesar's leash from Ben. 'You can leave him with us, Sergeant. We'll take tiptop care of him.'

Ben looked down at Caesar, who looked right back up at him with pleading eyes. Ben always dreaded parting with his canine partner. Apart from the sadness he felt, he was wracked by guilt, even though he knew that this was the way things had to be. Dropping to one knee again, he gave Caesar another hug and a vigorous pat. 'Be a good soldier,' he said, 'and you'll soon be back home with Josh and Maddie and Nan and me.'

The mention of all the members of the Fulton family waiting for him back home in Australia set Caesar's tail wagging.

'That's it, mate. Enjoy your stay here.' Ben kissed the top of Caesar's head, then rose back to his feet and handed Caesar's leash to Joe. 'Take good care of him.'

'You got it, Sergeant. So, to be clear, you won't be coming back to collect Caesar when his stay here is over?'

'No, the San Antonio Police Department will be sending someone to collect him and take him to the airport for the flight back to Australia.'

'Got it, and of course we'll organise all the veterinary checks and clearances for his trip back Down Under.'

Ben looked at Caesar. 'Sit!' he commanded. And Caesar immediately sat. 'Caesar, stay!' To emphasise the command, Ben pointed his index finger at Caesar.

Caesar returned his gaze with a pleading look that seemed to say, *Don't leave me here, boss. I want to go with you.*

'Be a good boy for Joe, and I'll see you soon.' Ben turned and strode to the door, deliberately stopping himself from looking back. He knew that if he did, it would make leaving more difficult.

Caesar watched the door as it closed behind Ben. He felt the tug on his leash and rose to follow Joe, his tail down.

'Come, and I'll introduce you to all your new buddies,' said Joe. 'Having said that, you'll be in quarantine, so there'll be no fraternising. You get a room all to yourself in the quarantine wing.'

CHAPTER 10

After travelling for close to twenty-four hours, Ben walked through the door at 3 Kokoda Crescent in Holsworthy, New South Wales. Just as he let his kitbag sag from his shoulder and slip to the floor, an unfamiliar sound met his ears – the pounding of drums. He walked along the corridor to investigate and stopped at the door to his son's bedroom. Ben opened the door.

Josh was seated at a drum kit that had been crammed into his room beside his bed. With earphones in, Josh was singing off-key and drumming along to a tune playing on his iPod. Looking up, he saw his bemused father standing in the doorway, and grinned.

A knowing smile spread across Ben's face. With a wave, he withdrew and closed the door.

'Daddy! You're back from special-opping!'

Ben turned to see Maddie running toward him. 'Princess!' he said, scooping her up in his arms. 'Yes, I'm back,' he said, almost shouting to be heard over Josh's drumming. 'Minus Caesar, sadly. But we'll have him back with us before long.'

'Poor Caesar,' Maddie said. 'I bet he misses us. Is his doggy hotel nice?'

'Yes, he'll get the best of care there,' Ben assured her.

Maddie frowned. 'Daddy, I'm worried about him. I was looking at some pictures I took the night before you both went away. Can I show you?'

'Sure.' Puzzled, Ben set her down on her feet.

She led him to her bedroom and brought up the photos on her phone. 'See. Caesar looks evil. As if the Devil has professed him.'

'Where did you hear about the Devil possessing people?' Ben asked, inspecting the picture of Caesar. He appeared to be in Maddie's room in the dark and his eyes glowed red.

'On TV. People's heads spin all the way around and everything!'

'That's just made-up stuff,' said Ben. 'It doesn't really happen. All dogs' eyes glow in the dark like that if light shines into them, Maddie. A membrane called the tapetum sits behind a dog's eye. It reflects light and helps the retina register light that enters the eye. That's why dogs can see at least four times better at night than we can.'

'*Four* times better?' said Maddie, impressed. 'So, Caesar isn't professed by the Devil?'

Ben couldn't help but chuckle. 'No, Caesar isn't possessed by the Devil. He's just got different eyes to us.'

'It's like he's got a superpower.'

'I suppose you're right.' In the background, Josh was still pounding the drums. 'Let's go see what Nan's up to.' Ben took Maddie into his arms and carried her to the kitchen, where Nan sat waiting for a cake to bake.

Nan smiled and laid aside her magazine. 'Home again, home again, jiggity-jig,' she said.

'When did that happen?' Ben said, nodding toward Josh's bedroom. He set Maddie back on her feet. 'He's good. Where'd the drum kit come from?' He closed the kitchen door behind him, shutting out the noise.

'I hired it for him. He'd love one of his own,' said Nan. 'He's started a band at school with Baxter Chung, Kelvin Corbett and a very nice boy called Ash, who is the lead vocalist.'

'The singer, Nan,' Maddie corrected.

'The singer,' said Nan, winking at Ben.

'This is all news to me,' said Ben, sagging down into a chair.

'You have been away a lot lately. And Josh wanted to surprise you.'

'He surprised me, all right,' Ben said with a chuckle.

'And Caesar is in quarantine in the US?' said Nan.

Ben nodded wearily.

'I think it's silly that Caesar has to be quaramteemed,'

said Maddie. 'Why don't people have to be quaram-teemed when they go to other countries, too? We can catch diseases and bring them back, can't we?'

'We can, and do, all the time,' said Ben. 'And years ago people were regularly quarantined when major epidemics broke out. That was before air travel took over from sea travel as the main mode of transport. But these days we all expect to come and go without delay. Imagine having to be stuck in quarantine for ten or fourteen days every time you got off a plane from overseas.'

'But if it stopped people from being sick . . .' Maddie reasoned.

Ben shrugged. 'It's the price we pay for the ability to travel anywhere at any time. But at least when Caesar comes back we'll know for sure that he isn't sick.'

Maddie thought for a moment. 'Does he have TV in his hotel?'

Ben smiled at Nan as he answered. 'Er, no TV.'

'Poor Caesar,' said Maddie. 'What about Skype? Could we talk to him on Skype, like we do when you're on ops? That way, he wouldn't be so lonely.'

'You know, Mads, I did think about setting up some Skype sessions with Caesar.'

'Goody!' she cried.

'But Caesar isn't that into technology. He doesn't know how Skype works.'

'Who does?' Nan laughed. 'I'm still struggling to understand how electricity works.'

'Yes, but Caesar would hear our voices, and not know where they were coming from,' said Ben. 'I think it would confuse him too much. He would expect us to be somewhere close by if he heard us.'

'It's different when your dad is there with Caesar and we talk to them both on Skype, Maddie,' said Nan. 'Your dad's presence makes up for us not being there.'

'And we don't want to make him fret any more than we can help, do we?' added Ben.

'I suppose not.' Maddie sighed. 'Poor Caesar is all alone.'

'He's got plenty of company, don't worry,' her father assured her. 'And he'll soon be home with us.'

CHAPTER 11

The following Monday, Ben reported for duty at the Special Operations Engineer Regiment's EDD training centre. This was located adjacent to the army base at Holsworthy in New South Wales, southwest of Sydney. Because Ben was based there, he and his family had lived in Holsworthy since before Maddie was born.

It was always hard for Ben to readjust to routine military life without Caesar. Whenever he had to leave his EDD in a quarantine facility following a deployment, Ben would return to base at Holsworthy and be assigned to the training of new explosive detection dogs and their handlers. With dogs and handlers retiring regularly and leaving army service, or occasionally becoming casualties on operations, there was a constant need for new recruits in the EDD department.

Sometimes Ben's training assignment involved a new dog working with an experienced handler. Other times he had to work with a new handler and a dog fresh from civilian sources. Both would be going through EDD training together. It wasn't just a matter of training the dog. The handler had to be trained in EDD techniques, too. On this occasion, Ben's assignment was to oversee the training of Lance Corporal Matthew Dunn and his dog. The fair-headed Dunn was twenty-two and had entered the Australian Army with the ambition of working with war dogs. Once he'd completed his army basic training, his wish was granted and he was assigned to the SOER for EDD training.

On arrival, he was matched with a black kelpie named Queenie. This first Monday of Ben's new assignment, he watched Dunn and Queenie work with five other army handlers and novice dogs on the training ground at Holsworthy. Queenie proved bright and eager. However, while Dunn was equally eager, he was uncertain with Queenie, leaving the dog confused about what was expected of her. Ben saw that he would have his work cut out turning this pair into a team. But at least the task helped to take Ben's mind off Caesar, who he was missing terribly.

🐾🐾

Cindy Levine was deep in conversation with one of the Doghouse's handlers when two male police officers walked into the lobby.

'Hi there,' Cindy said with a smile. 'What can I do for you this fine day, officers?'

'We are here for the dog,' said one of the policemen, jamming his thumbs in his gun belt.

Cindy's smile wavered. 'And what dog would that be?'

'César,' the second policeman replied in a heavy Hispanic accent.

'Caesar, the Australian war dog?' Cindy responded with surprise. 'We were told that he was to be picked up only when his quarantine period was over, and that's not for quite a while yet.'

'Lady, we only follow orders,' said the first policeman, sounding agitated, 'and our orders are to pick up the dog called César.'

'Oh.' Cindy turned to her computer and brought up Caesar's file. At the bottom it said, 'To be collected by SAPD.' Cindy returned her attention to the two policemen, still unsure of what to do. 'We were expecting Caesar to be collected by the Police Department . . . but only at the end of his quarantine period. I'll need to run this by my grandfather, just to be on the safe side.' She picked up the phone.

'Do we gotta put handcuffs on the dog to take him in?' said the second cop.

'Just hold your horses, officer,' Cindy said patiently.

'What horses?' the first policeman asked, sounding confused.

'Just bear with me,' said Cindy, trying not to let the two men fluster her. 'Let me call his cellphone.'

'We ain't got all day,' said the second policeman. 'Just give us the dog.'

Cindy quickly dialled her grandfather's number but was directed straight to voicemail. 'Hi, Pops, it's me,' she said. 'Just leaving a message to say that the SAPD is here to collect Caesar. It all seems okay, just a lot earlier than I was expecting. Give me a call if there's a problem.'

'You gonna release the dog into our custody or not?' the second policeman pressed. 'Or should we take you in for obstructing police officers in the course of their duty?'

'Yeah,' said the first policeman. 'Like my *compadre* say, you are obstructing police officers doing their duty.'

'There's no need for that, officers,' Cindy responded anxiously. 'I'm only doing my job. I'm sure that everything is fine. Wait here, and I'll get Caesar for you.' She turned to a handler she'd been talking with previously. 'Mandy, keep an eye on the phone while I'm gone, will you?'

After a few minutes Cindy returned with Caesar trotting along beside her. Caesar's tail was wagging slowly; any chance for some exercise and interaction with humans was pleasing to him and would set his tail wagging. He hoped the humans might be interested in playing games with him the way that he and Ben played. He missed the games as much as he missed Ben.

'This is the dog César?' asked policeman number one.

'Uh-huh,' Cindy replied, offering the leash to him. 'I'll need you to sign him out.'

'Sure thing,' said policeman number two, smiling for the first time. 'Where do we sign?'

Caesar looked up at policeman number one, who was holding the end of his leash. His tail stilled. Caesar didn't like the look or the smell of the man. If need be, Caesar could identify every individual on the planet via their aroma, because every person has their own specific odour. In part, that odour is dictated by what they eat. The rest has to do with a variety of other factors ranging from the state of a person's health to their personal hygiene. Caesar could also tell from a person's body odour whether they were happy or sad, or whether they were friendly or unfriendly. This guy in the police uniform was definitely giving off an unfriendly odour.

Cindy held up the release form. 'Which one of you is signing?'

'Here,' said policeman number two, taking the sheet of paper. 'I'll sign.' He glanced over the page, then said, holding out one hand, 'I'll need to borrow a pen.'

Cindy, thinking it was strange for a policeman to be on duty without something to write with, grabbed a pen from her desk. 'There you go,' she said, handing it to him.

Policeman number two signed on the dotted line before handing the piece of paper and pen back to Cindy. 'Are we good to go now?' he asked.

'Sure, officer,' Cindy replied, glancing at the signature. She filed the sheet in a folder labelled 'Pending'.

'What about his stuff?' asked policeman number one. 'You know, his dog things.'

Cindy frowned. 'Caesar doesn't have "dog things",' she replied. 'He is a working war dog, so he travels light. But I'll give you his dietary and exercise requirements.'

She quickly printed off the instructions, which policeman number two folded and slipped into his breast pocket.

'Okay, that's it,' he said. 'We're outta here.' He turned and walked toward the front door.

'Come on, dog,' said policeman number one, tugging roughly at Caesar's leash.

But Caesar would not budge. With a glint of defiance and suspicion in his eyes, he looked up at policeman number one.

Policeman number one glared down at him. 'Come on, dog!' he growled, tugging harder.

Policeman number two went over and pushed Caesar toward the door with the heel of his boot. Caesar looked around and bared his teeth at him, a low growl rumbling in the back of his throat. Policeman number one tugged even harder, dragging Caesar toward the door.

'It's okay, Caesar,' Cindy called reassuringly. At least, she hoped everything was okay. She didn't like these two cops, and Caesar didn't seem to like them either. But the cops had signed out the labrador, so there was nothing more she could do.

Eventually, the two men dragged Caesar outside and pushed him into the back of a white four-door pick-up truck. They secured his leash to a rail running along the side of the pick-up's tray and slammed the tailgate shut. The pair then climbed into the cab and, with police-man number one at the wheel, departed. Caesar stood in the rear looking forlornly back at the facility they were rapidly leaving behind.

Cindy watched from the window until Caesar and the pick-up were out of sight. Something didn't feel right to her, but before she could think about it further the phone rang. 'Good morning, Joe's Doghouse, Cindy speaking,' she answered. 'How may I help you today?'

'Hi there, honey, it's me,' said Joe. 'What's this about the cops coming to collect Caesar?'

'Oh, it turned out to be nothing, Pops. The SAPD came and took Caesar away,' she replied. 'They signed a release and all.'

'The SAPD took Caesar?' Joe sounded confused. 'Why? He can't go back to Australia yet.'

'Maybe they're going to use Caesar here in the States,' Cindy suggested.

'Yeah, maybe. But no one told me they were coming for him early. You say they signed for him? What was the name of the officer who signed?'

'Hold on.' Cindy retrieved the form signed by policeman number two and read the signature. 'Officer Antonio Santa Maria.'

'Antonio Santa Maria? Okay. I'll check with Captain De Silva at the SAPD.'

'Okay,' said Cindy, her sense of unease returning. 'Do you think Caesar's all right, Pops?'

'I'm sure it'll be fine, Cindy. I'll call you back once I've spoken with the captain.'

The white pick-up inched its way along in bumper-to-bumper traffic on Interstate 35 heading south to the Mexican border from San Antonio. Policeman number one and policeman number two were no longer in SAPD uniform. They now wore casual shirts, blue jeans, cowboy boots and big Stetson hats with wide brims that curved skyward. The pick-up's registration plates had been changed, its Texan plates swapped for Mexican ones issued by the state of Nuevo León. Both men were chattering in Spanish and laughing while Caesar stood in the tray, studying the scene. Finally it came their turn to show their papers to an agent of US Customs and Border Protection at the Laredo border post.

'Enjoy your stay?' asked the agent. He peered into the cab before checking their vehicle permit and visitor cards.

'Just a little visit,' the driver replied. 'But, *sí*, it was good.'

'Uh-huh.' The border agent looked in the back, satisfying himself that the rear was empty except for the labrador. 'Nice-looking dog.'

The passenger of the pick-up smiled.

'Hold on.' The border guard took the papers to another officer. Blank-faced, the second border agent checked the details on computer, then stamped the paperwork. When these two men had crossed the border from Mexico early that morning, they had not been travelling with a dog. But that was not recorded on the documentation, and the fact they now had a dog with them didn't raise so much as an eyebrow. The US Government's focus was on what was being brought *into* the country, rather than what was being taken out. The Customs and Border Protection agent handed the papers back to the driver. 'Have a nice day.'

The driver grinned. 'We will be sure to do that, *amigo*.'

The pick-up eased forward. As it did, Caesar looked at the agent, who smiled at him as he passed. Labradors don't bark a lot, and Caesar hardly ever barked, but now he began to. Loudly, insistently, he barked at the US border agent, as if to say, *These guys are kidnapping me!*

'Yeah, yeah, same to you, crazy mutt,' said the border agent. He turned his attention to the next vehicle in the line.

Metres ahead, the white pick-up came to a halt at the Mexican border post. After the Mexican border guards were satisfied, the pick-up drove on, and the two men in the cabin roared with laughter. Caesar, silent once again, glumly stretched out on the ribbed metal floor and rested his jaw on his front paws. He didn't know it, but he was now in Mexico, and heading south for Monterrey.

It was in the early hours of the morning when Ben's phone began to ring. Ben was awake in an instant. Flicking on the bedside lamp and sitting up, he checked the time: 3.03. Then he picked up his phone and saw that it was an unidentified caller. 'Ben Fulton,' he answered. 'Who's this?'

'Hi there, Sergeant. This is Captain Leo De Silva of the San Antonio Police Department. How are you doing?'

'Well, Captain, considering that it's three in the morning here and I was fast asleep . . .'

'Oh, sorry about that, Sergeant. Are you ahead of us folks in Texas, or behind?'

'Ahead,' Ben answered impatiently. 'What can I do for you, Captain?'

'I sorta got some bad news for you.'

Ben frowned. 'Bad news? What kind of bad news?'

'Well, you see, we kinda lost Caesar.' There was an embarrassed tone in his voice.

For a moment, Ben thought that he was hearing things. '*Lost* Caesar? How could you lose him? He's at Joe's Doghouse. I checked him in there myself.'

'Caesar's not there anymore,' said De Silva. 'Two guys posing as SAPD officers collected him this morning. We've found the SAPD uniforms they used, burned in an oil drum behind a gas station on the I-35.'

Ben had gone cold all over. Very much awake now, he threw his feet over the edge of the bed and sat bolt upright. 'That doesn't make sense. Who would want to steal Caesar?'

'I dunno. But an immigration officer at Laredo remembers seeing a healthy-looking brown labrador at the border-crossing this afternoon. He was in the back of a pick-up that matches the description of the vehicle the abductors used. It looks like Caesar could be in Mexico.'

Ben decided to save all his questions for later. There was no time to lose, and a single thought dominated his mind – he had to get Caesar back. 'I'll be on the next flight out.'

CHAPTER 12

In one of the most rundown neighbourhoods in the city of Monterrey, the white pick-up truck made its way along a rubbish-strewn, unpaved backstreet. Here, a mob of barefoot children were yelling and playing soccer with the earnestness of seasoned professionals. From the back of the truck, Caesar, standing and unsteady on his feet, surveyed the scene unhappily. The children paid him no heed; there were plenty of dogs in this neighbourhood. They scampered across the dirt, imagining they were playing for Mexico in the World Cup. The children dodged and dribbled and dreamed of firing wickedly curving balls toward an imaginary net at the end of the street, scoring goals that would transform them into national sporting heroes.

The white pick-up drew to a halt in front of a solid metal gate, flanked on either side by high concrete walls. A CCTV camera high atop a gatepost zeroed in on the vehicle. The driver leaned out of the open window and, grinning, gave a 'V' for victory sign to the camera. With a shudder, the solid metal gate opened and the pick-up rolled through it.

East of the forecourt rose a grim four-storey concrete building. It was built around a central courtyard that housed a palatial swimming pool. It also had an American-style basement garage, and metal shutters adorned all its windows.

Just as the driver and passenger were climbing out of the pick-up, two members of the Árbol cartel emerged from a side door off the garage. They were wearing baseball caps, jeans and loose shirts, and armed with snub-nosed Heckler & Koch MP5 submachine guns. With fingers close to the triggers of their weapons, they watched the gate close. A cheer rose from the boys in the street – a goal had just been scored.

From a watchtower on the roof, more Árbol guards kept watch over the scene with their M16 rifles at the ready. Once the gate shuddered to a close, one of the garage doors rolled up with a metallic clatter and a hum. A tubby man with an ugly scar down the left side of his face emerged and walked up the slope from the garage.

'Vargas, my friend.' The driver of the pick-up smiled. 'We have that little gift for *el padrino* that you asked us to collect in Texas.' He walked around to the rear of the vehicle.

'I see that, Diego, *amigo*,' Vargas said with delight, admiring Caesar. 'Good job, *compadre*. Good job.'

Standing in the back of the pick-up, Caesar regarded Vargas with suspicion.

Diego lowered the tailgate while his partner, Tommy, unfastened Caesar's leash. With a tug of the leash, Caesar reluctantly moved to the end of the tray. He sat down, looking unhappily at the ground. Diego reached into the back of the pick-up, took out a large sombrero and placed it on Caesar's head. He then removed his sunglasses and placed them over Caesar's eyes. The sight of the dog wearing a sombrero and sunglasses brought roars of laughter from the men.

'I get a photo,' said Diego, taking out his phone. 'Me and César the wonder dog.' He leaned in close to the labrador and took a selfie.

Again, the men laughed. Caesar, knowing they were laughing at him, abruptly lowered his head, sending the sombrero flying and the sunglasses sliding from his nose.

'Here, doggy!' said Vargas, patting his leg. 'Jump down here to me.'

As Diego recovered his sunglasses, Tommy tugged hard on the leash, but still Caesar resisted leaving the back of the vehicle.

'Come, César,' said Vargas. 'Chow time.'

Caesar recognised the word 'chow'. He and Ben had mixed with plenty of American soldiers over the past few years for both of them to become familiar with their term for food. Tempted by the mention of chow, Caesar jumped down to the ground and, with his tail wagging slowly, looked at Vargas expectantly.

Vargas patted Caesar and bent to take a look at his collar, which had a metal ID tag on it with his name inscribed. 'Okay, César,' he said, smiling broadly, 'we will now present you to *el padrino*.' He took hold of Caesar's leash. 'Come.'

Caesar allowed himself to be led into the building via the massive ground-floor garage. It was filled with vehicles including a black Hummer four-wheel drive, a red Ferrari 435 sports car, a yellow Porsche Cayenne – all the property of El Loro Verde and paid for by the proceeds of crime. The men and Caesar crowded into a lift and made their way to the top floor.

The lift doors slid open to reveal a tall woman with blonde hair wearing a tight pink dress and holding a dog the size of a rat. The dog, a chihuahua, had been dyed pink from head to toe. At the sight of Caesar, it began to bark at him, squirming in the woman's arms.

'Hush, Rosa! Hush!' the woman urged, firming her grip on the chihuahua. She pressed her face against its head. 'Do not worry, I will not allow the big brown dog to hurt you,' she crooned, then turned to glare at the three men. 'What is *that* thing doing here?' she demanded, nodding toward Caesar.

'*El padrino* asked for it, Lola,' said Vargas.

'You do not call me Lola in front of people, Vargas,' she growled, as a severe frown furrowed her brow.

Vargas shrugged. 'Sorry. But you are my sister, after all.'

'You must call me Señora Marron. I am El Loro Verde's wife, not just some commoner.'

'Okay, okay.' Vargas sighed. 'But at least keep the rat quiet. You know how *el padrino* hates barking, Señora Marron.'

'Hush, Rosa, my sweet,' said Lola, stepping into the lift.

Caesar accompanied Vargas, looking up at Rosa as Lola passed by with the chihuahua in her arms. He had never seen a dog like her before in his life. The lift doors shut, and Lola and the chihuahua were gone. Now he looked around the room, wondering if Ben might be here someplace to take him off the hands of these strangers.

'Are you ready for a surprise, *Padrino*?' Vargas called, leading Caesar into the massive living room which occupied much of the top floor.

Diego and his companion, expecting a big reward from their boss, followed along behind.

Carlos Marron, the Green Parrot, lay on a black leather sofa watching a quiz show. 'It was *Blue Hawaii*, you idiot!' he yelled at the television. 'Elvis sang "Can't Help Falling in Love" in the movie *Blue Hawaii*!'

He groaned and looked around at his three henchmen. 'I must have seen that movie a hundred times, Vargas,' he said. 'It was the King's best.'

'*Sí, Padrino,*' Vargas replied, leading Caesar into his boss's view. 'I have the dog for you.'

Marron's eyes dropped to the brown labrador at his lieutenant's side. 'What is this?'

'This, *Padrino*, is César the exploding dog,' said Vargas proudly. 'As you ordered.'

Marron leaned forward to study Caesar. '*This* is the bomb-sniffing dog?' he asked. 'Looks like any old dog to me. Are you sure this is the one that was on the television, Vargas?'

'*Sí, Padrino.* This is the dog that smells the bombs. Diego and Tommy got him from the dog's home in San Antonio, where he was being kept. If you look at his collar, it says his name and "Australian Army". This is without question the dog, *Padrino.*'

'Okay,' said Marron. 'And I asked you to get me this dog so that it would sniff any bombs that Estrella planted to kill me or my family. Correct?'

Diego beamed. '*Sí, Padrino.* And here it is.'

'And how is the dog going to tell me there is a bomb?'

Diego's smile faded. '*Padrino?* I do not understand.'

'The dog – he sniffs a bomb. How is he going to tell me that he has found a bomb and where he has found it?'

Diego looked baffled.

'Is this a talking dog? Is that what you are telling me –
this is a dog that can talk?' demanded the crime boss.

Diego laughed awkwardly. 'No, *Padrino*. The dog
cannot talk. That would be something, wouldn't it –'

'What use is this dog to me then?'

Diego looked both embarrassed and afraid. 'Er . . .'

'The dog and the Australian soldier on the television – they are a team, you idiots! Without the soldier,
the dog cannot do its job. The soldier is the only one
who knows when the dog finds a bomb. The dog has a
way of telling him. But what is that way?' Marron glared
at Vargas. 'Do you know what it is?'

'No, *Padrino*, not exactly,' Vargas confessed, unable to
look his boss in the eye.

'Why did you not get me the dog's handler as well,
you imbecile?'

Vargas's look of self-satisfaction quickly disappeared.
'The dog's handler has returned to Australia. It was not
possible –'

'Get me a human who can understand the bomb-
sniffing dog, Vargas!' Marron raged, yelling at the top of
his voice. 'Do you hear me? All of you?' He cast a fierce
glance around all three of his henchmen.

'*Sí, Padrino*,' Vargas, Diego and Tommy chorused.

'Now, get out! And take that useless dog with you! I do
not wish to see it again unless you also bring me its handler.'

'*Sí, Padrino*,' the trio returned.

CHAPTER 13

'What do you mean Caesar has been taken, Daddy?' Maddie demanded from across the breakfast table.

'You're saying he's been dognapped?' Josh could hardly believe it. His spoon hovered over his cereal bowl. 'How?'

'Oh, Ben,' said Nan, her face ashen. 'Caesar is a member of this family. You have to get him back!'

'You don't have to tell me that, Mum,' said Ben. 'How do you think I feel, leaving Caesar there? He trusted me.'

Maddie looked at her father, then at her grandmother, with a lost expression on her face. 'I'm befuzzled.'

'Some bad people pretended to be policemen in order to steal Caesar, Maddie,' her father tried to explain.

'But why? What do they want him for?'

'Caesar is a valuable dog, Maddie,' said Nan. 'Perhaps they want a ransom for him.'

'What's a "ramson"?' Maddie queried.

'We would have to pay a lot of money to get him back,' said Josh. 'Right, Dad?'

Ben nodded. 'Right, son.'

'Oh, is that all?' said Maddie, sounding relieved. 'Then just give them the money. Caesar must be very frightened and missing us. You can have the money in my egg, Daddy, if you need it.'

'Thank you, princess.' Ben smiled for the first time since he'd received the news. 'I'm sure we won't have to break into your egg.'

A while back, Ben's journalist friend Amanda Ritchie had given Maddie a large egg-shaped money bank with 'For Your Nest Egg' printed on the side. Every time Maddie had a spare coin she would drop it in and listen with pleasure when she shook it. She was convinced that her savings in the egg must be approaching a million dollars by now.

'Do you think this could be about a ransom, Ben?' Nan asked.

'I don't know, Mum. The authorities in Texas are pretty sure that Caesar has been taken across the border into Mexico. If that's the case, it's probably the work of one of the Mexican crime cartels. They often kidnap high-profile people in Mexico and demand a lot of money for their return.'

'And Caesar is famous,' said Josh.

Ben nodded. 'He is famous, and he was on TV after the bomb blast in San Antonio. Maybe one of the crime cartels saw him on TV and targeted him as a result. We'll have to wait and see if they make a ransom demand.'

At that moment, Ben's phone began to ring. Setting down his cup, Ben saw that it was Liberty Lee calling from the UN in New York. Excusing himself, he left to take her call.

'Yes, Captain, what can I do for you?' he answered.

'Sergeant Fulton, Major-General Jones of SOCOM has just informed me of Caesar's abduction,' said Liberty. 'I am very sorry to hear of it. So, too, is the Secretary-General.'

'Thank you,' said Ben. 'It came as a shock, I can tell you. I spoke to General Jones last night, after Captain De Silva called, and he's given me permission to return to Texas at once.'

'That is good. The Secretary-General has asked me to tell you that, should the need arise for Caesar to be extricated from the hands of those who are holding him, he is prepared to call upon GRRR. We have already put GRRR team members on standby, in readiness for a rescue mission once details of Caesar's whereabouts are known.'

'That's really good of you, ma'am, and the Secretary-General,' Ben said gratefully, 'but let's hope it won't come to that.'

'Keep me informed.'

'I will. Thank you, Captain. I really appreciate your support. My whole family does.'

'We would do this if any member of GRRR was in

trouble, Sergeant. And Caesar is just as important as any other member of the team.'

'Yes, he is, ma'am.'

'He was separated from you once before, was he not?'

'Yes, ma'am, during a battle with the Taliban in Afghanistan. It took us fourteen months to get him back that time.'

'I'm sure it will not take so long this time. Good luck.'

Ben hung up, and found himself pondering why fate had done this to him a second time. Returning to the kitchen, he was determined to keep the mood light. He was angry at the way the quarantine facility had handed his dog over to the kidnappers, and he was fearful for Caesar's safety, but he had to keep his family's spirits up.

'All good,' he said as he returned to the table. 'Finish your breakfast and I'll run you both to school.'

'Caesar is going to be all right, isn't he, Daddy?' asked Maddie, toying absently with her cereal.

'Absolutely, princess,' Ben assured her. 'I'll be flying out this afternoon to track him down.'

'When do you think we can get him back?' Josh asked. He felt guilty for not paying more attention to Caesar just before he went away.

Ben didn't rush to reply. His training as a soldier had capitalised on his nature as a practical and methodical man. 'Let's work on the basis that I'm going to locate Caesar and get him back on the quarantine program,' he replied. 'In which case, we'll have him home pretty much around the same time as we were expecting originally. Okay?'

Maddie smiled. She trusted her father and took his word for it. 'Okay,' she said, before taking another scoop of cereal.

Ben looked at her brother. 'Okay, Josh?'

Josh nodded. 'Okay.'

'The UN has promised that, if necessary, GRRR will be deployed to rescue Caesar,' added Ben.

This brought a smile to Josh's face. 'Cool. That's great, Dad.'

Ben patted Josh on the shoulder. 'It is great, mate. And GRRR has never failed on a mission.'

Nan smiled across the table at Ben. She knew how deeply he must be hurting. 'Yes, we'll soon have Caesar back,' she said.

It was a statement filled with as much hope as it was confidence.

🐾🐾

Caesar sat looking at his captors. Vargas had cleared El Loro Verde's garage of its cars. All the vehicles now stood out in the forecourt at the front of the compound. On the garage floor, Vargas had set out four large cardboard boxes two metres apart. Diego and Tommy, as well as several of El Loro's bodyguards, had come to watch.

'Come, César,' said Vargas, unhitching Caesar's leash from a pipe running along the wall, and leading him to the cardboard boxes. When Vargas came to a halt, Caesar came to a halt beside him. 'We do not need a handler for you,' Vargas said. 'You will show me the bomb the same way the dogs in airports identify contraband. I have seen them do it. Here before you, César, are four boxes. In one of the boxes I have planted some sticks of gelignite. I want you to tell me which box the explosive sticks are in.'

With his head cocked to one side, Caesar looked up at Vargas with an expression on his face that seemed to say, *What are you talking about, mister?*

'The dog would only understand English, Vargas,' called Tommy, watching with folded arms.

'Okay, okay,' Vargas acknowledged. 'Your English is better than mine. You come tell the dog what I want it to do, in English.'

Tommy ambled over. 'Okay, César,' he said, looking down at the labrador, 'Vargas here wants you to find the explosives in one of these boxes. *Comprende?*'

Caesar looked dumbly from Tommy to Vargas and back again.

Tommy pointed at the boxes. 'You find the bomb in the box. Okay?'

'Find the boom-boom, César,' Vargas added, in his heavily accented English. 'Find the boom-boom!'

What neither Tommy nor Vargas knew was that Caesar only went into bomb-sniffing mode upon hearing a specific command. That two-word command was common to all dogs trained for the Australian Army's Special Operations Engineer Regiment. Without it, Caesar would not do as Vargas wanted.

Impatiently tugging on the leash, Vargas led Caesar past the four cardboard boxes and back the other way again. Caesar watched Vargas all the way, suspicious of what the man might do to him at any moment. Wary and confused, Caesar sat down beside Vargas and looked absently around the garage. Besides, routinely associating the smell of explosives with Ben and the 'games' they played together, he was not in EDD mode.

Vargas turned to Tommy and Diego. 'You did get the right dog?' he said accusingly. 'Could there be some mistake?'

'Sí, is the right dog, Vargas,' said Diego. 'There is no mistake.'

'It just needs the right master to operate it,' said Tommy. In the background, the bodyguards were laughing at Vargas.

'Okay, okay,' Vargas said irritably. 'Then we need to find a dog handler. One who knows how to make these sniffing dogs work.'

'The police have such dogs,' said Diego.

'And the army,' added Tommy.

'Then you two will get me a police or army dog handler,' said Vargas, leading Caesar back to where the labrador had spent the night. 'Pay them or threaten them – just get them here.'

Tommy raised his eyebrows. 'You want us to kidnap a dog handler now?' he asked.

'Finish the job,' Vargas called back. 'You should have brought the dog's handler with this animal. What use is one without the other?'

'You did not tell us to get the handler too,' said Diego defensively.

'And César's handler has gone back to Australia,' said Tommy.

Vargas waved them away and began fastening Caesar's leash to a pipe on the wall. 'Just get someone who can make this dog find bombs. *Vámonos!*'

'Okay, okay,' said Diego, turning for the door.

'We always have to clean up his messes,' Tommy mumbled, keeping his voice low so that only Diego could hear him.

Diego nodded. 'If Vargas were not Lola's brother, *el padrino* would not even bother with such a fool.'

'What are you saying?' said Vargas.

'We were saying that we will have a fool of a dog handler for you within twenty-four hours, Vargas,' Tommy replied.

'Good. Good.'

As Diego and Tommy set off on their mission, the Green Parrot's cars were all returned to their parking places. The garage doors were shut, leaving Caesar alone. Settling down on the floor, he rested his jaw on his paws and closed his eyes. This garage was now his prison.

CHAPTER 14

Captain De Silva was there to meet Ben at San Antonio International Airport. 'Ben, I can't tell you how sorry we are about what happened to Caesar,' he said as they walked to the car. 'You must be real shook up by all this.'

'My whole family is,' Ben replied. 'It's like we've lost one of our children.'

'I blame Joe Levine's granddaughter,' said De Silva, sounding genuinely angry. 'Levine's a top operator. He used to handle service dogs for the SAPD, and before that for the Marine Corps. If he'd been around when the cartel's hoods turned up he wouldn't have let Caesar out of his sight. Cindy Levine's lucky we haven't charged her.'

'Charged her with what?'

'We would have thought of something. But my chief doesn't want the story to get out. If we charged her, Caesar's abduction would be in the media in a flash.'

'Too embarrassing for your department?' said Ben.

De Silva shrugged. 'Right now our focus is on tracking Caesar down.'

'My commanding general also wants to keep Caesar's abduction confidential for now,' Ben advised. 'We don't want his kidnappers to know we're onto them. Tell me, where did the crooks get the police uniforms and ID?'

'They could have hired them from a costume shop or bought them from a manufacturer. The rest could be mocked up pretty easily. Problem was, Cindy Levine didn't ask to see these guys' ID.' De Silva shook his head. 'How dumb was that? Your government should sue the Levines.'

Ben shook his head. 'I don't want to sue anyone. I just want Caesar back.'

They reached the car and Ben slid into the back.

Sergeant Austin was behind the wheel. 'Sorry to see you again under these circumstances,' he said, turning around to face Ben.

'Have you got any idea where Caesar is?' Ben asked.

'We think he's in Mexico,' replied De Silva. 'We've secured a CCTV image from the border post at Laredo of a brown labrador in the back of a pick-up entering Nuevo León. It could be Caesar. It's the only sighting we've had.'

'Where in Mexico would they take him?'

'Monterrey's our bet,' said Austin, starting the engine.

'We think Caesar was kidnapped by one of the cartels,' said De Silva, 'for ransom.'

'Have the kidnappers made contact with a ransom demand?' Ben asked.

De Silva grimaced. 'Not yet.'

'How long do the cartels usually wait to make a ransom demand after they carry out a kidnapping?'

'Usually between twenty-four and forty-eight hours,' De Silva advised.

'I see.' More than forty-eight hours had passed since Caesar's abduction, and Ben was uneasy. 'So, it's not necessarily a kidnap for ransom we're looking at?' he said, thinking aloud.

'I guess not,' De Silva conceded, 'but why else would they take Caesar?'

'Maybe they like what one particularly clever labrador can do,' Ben surmised.

Beside him, De Silva looked bemused. 'Come again?'

'Caesar is the most famous explosive detection dog in the world. Right?'

'Right. But . . .'

'And we had two car bombs here in San Antonio, one of which Caesar detected.'

'Yeah . . .'

'So, ask yourself "what if."'

'Huh?' De Silva wasn't following.

'What if someone wants Caesar to protect them from car bombs – from IEDs?' said Ben.

'Hell's bells, partner, I think you're onto something!' De Silva exclaimed. 'It adds up.'

'Are the cartel bosses that smart?' asked Sergeant Austin.

'They could be that paranoid,' said De Silva, 'thinking the opposition is coming after them with a bomb, just like they did with Rocky Marron.'

Austin shook his head, unconvinced. 'Every cartel member I've come across has got tacos for brains.'

'One of those guys is just crazy enough to try something like this,' De Silva declared.

'Has the Mexican Government caught many of the cartel bosses in the past?' Ben asked.

'Over the last five or six years, with the military involved, they've locked away maybe fourteen or fifteen cartel bosses. We've put another two behind bars here in Texas.'

They drove to SAPD Headquarters on South Santa Rosa Avenue. There, in the captain's top-floor office, De Silva handed Ben a photograph that had been taken at the Laredo border post several days earlier. It was a close-up of a white pick-up in a line of vehicles. The head of a large dark dog could be seen standing in its tray. Ben studied the picture carefully.

'It looks like Caesar,' said De Silva.

Ben nodded slowly. 'Could be,' he said, deep in thought, 'but it's too far away to be sure. What have you been able to find out about the pick-up?'

'We got Mexico's Federal Police – the Federales – on it. The plates were from a stolen vehicle of a different make and model. The Federales have been on the lookout in

Nuevo León for the pick-up with a brown labrador, but it's as if they've been swallowed up over there in Mexico.'

Ben sank into a chair. He'd been travelling for more than a day and he was suddenly hit with a wave of fatigue. 'It's like looking for a needle in a haystack,' he said dejectedly.

'Right now, we can't even find the haystack.'

Sergeant Austin arrived with three steaming cups. 'Is the Australian Government prepared to offer a reward for Caesar's return, Ben?' he asked, handing the Australian sergeant a coffee.

'Like the US, the Australian Government has a policy of not paying ransom demands,' Ben replied.

'So, are you just going to sit here in San Antonio and wait for news?' Austin queried. 'Could be a long wait.'

'No way,' said Ben. 'I plan to search for Caesar myself.'

'Hell, yes!' Da Silva slammed a fist on his desk. 'We gotta do something. Not sure what, but we gotta do something.'

'Okay,' said Austin, sounding sceptical. 'What happens if we somehow locate Caesar over there in Mexico. We don't have jurisdiction there. And I don't trust anyone else to go in and get the dog out.'

'Not a problem,' said Ben. 'The Secretary-General of the UN has placed GRRR on alert. If the need arises, GRRR will join me to go in and extract Caesar.'

De Silva raised his eyebrows. 'You got friends in high places.'

'Caesar has friends in high places,' Ben responded. 'Besides, he's an integral part of GRRR, and GRRR never leaves a team member behind.'

Sergeant Austin took a sip of his coffee. 'So, how were you planning to track down your dawg?'

'Let's start with the cartel bosses,' Ben suggested. He looked directly at De Silva. 'Captain, you said you think Caesar's been taken to Monterrey. Tell me about the Mexican crime bosses there – the ones you think might have ordered Caesar's abduction. Help me get a handle on these people, starting with Rocky Marron's brother.'

Da Silva nodded. 'You got it, Ben. I'll get our criminal intelligence section to set up a detailed briefing for you.'

Enrico Vargas stood in the garage looking at Caesar. 'What's the matter with you? Eat!' Squatting down, he pointed to the plate he had placed in front of the labrador. 'Here. Very tasty. It's *birria*. I had it for dinner myself.'

Caesar sniffed the meat on the plate, then looked at Vargas with an expression that seemed to say, *That's not for me, mister.*

'It's beef. That's what dogs eat, isn't it?' Vargas was becoming increasingly frustrated. 'Come on, César, you must eat.'

But Caesar was totally disinterested in the dish. He lay down with his head on his front paws and watched Vargas carefully.

'I also cannot eat when I am away from home. Are you lonely, *amigo*?'

Caesar sneezed in response. *Birria*, an expensive delicacy in Mexico, was made with a base of dried roasted chilli peppers and also included a host of ingredients such as garlic. That chilli pepper base was tickling Caesar's nose. As hungry as he was, there was no way in the world he was going to eat a chilli dish. Plain, unadulterated beef was what he was used to. But virtually everything eaten by Vargas, and most other Mexicans, had chilli in it. Never having had a pet dog in his life, Vargas had no comprehension of what dogs ate.

Leaving the plate of food in case Caesar changed his mind, Vargas took the lift to the top floor. He found Lola in the kitchen cleaning up after dinner. After remodelling the kitchen on an expensive design Lola had seen in *Architectural Digest*, the oven sat unused. Instead, Lola spent her days sunning herself by the pool and, because money was no object, she ordered in food every day.

'Lola, you have to help me,' Vargas said to his sister. 'I have been reduced to looking after a dog! I had an important job in the Mexican Army before your brother convinced me to work for him – a very *skilled* job. It's not right that I should have to clean up after a dog.'

'You didn't need much convincing to come and work for Carlos, Enrico. He pays you ten times more than the army did,' replied his sister, wiping the granite benchtop. 'And don't come to me complaining about cleaning up after the dog. *You* screwed up. You didn't get the guy that was in charge of the smelling dog. So you fix things, and El Loro Verde will be happy with you again. It's simple, little brother.' She headed for the pantry.

'It's not simple, Lola,' he protested, following her. 'I've got Diego and Tommy looking for a dog handler, one who can talk to César in dog language, but these dog people don't grow on trees. And César has gone off his food – he would not touch the *birria*. I think he is lonely.'

'Lonely?' Lola laughed.

'Sure. Let him play with Rosa.'

Lola looked horrified. 'Are you crazy? He would *eat* Rosa!'

'I would watch them to make sure that Rosa is okay, trust me. We cannot have César being unhappy. We need him to find bombs.'

'What is the point of him finding bombs if you don't know when he has found them?'

'One problem at a time, sister. Diego and Tommy will find a handler. But first we must keep César happy. And if we keep César happy, we keep El Loro happy. *Sí?*'

Lola shrugged. 'It's your problem.'

'Well, maybe you can give me some of the special American dog food you get in for Rosa.'

Rosa enjoyed the most expensive dog food that money could buy. It was produced in California especially for the pampered pets of Hollywood movie stars. Lola had it flown in by the carton-load from the US for her pink chihuahua.

'You are not getting any of Rosa's food for that smelling dog,' she said defiantly. 'And you can forget about him playing with Rosa. She is a high-class dog and will not be having anything to do with your common working dog. You understand me, little brother?'

Vargas sighed. '*Sí*, you make life very hard for me, Lola.'

Sergeant Juanita Del Ray yawned as she stepped out of her police van. She had been on duty since before dawn, and it had been a long, hot, humid day. But now her workday was over. The sun had gone down and with it came the cool of evening. Juanita checked her watch and nodded to herself. She had time before she had to head home. A single mother, Juanita earned good money by Mexican standards. To earn that money, she had to work long hours, and every now and then she needed time to unwind after a tough day like today.

She walked over to the restaurant across the road. The rundown establishment, which was in need of fresh paint and new fittings, was crowded with football fans following a game on a large TV screen.

'Viva the striped ones!' Juanita called. Her local team, FC Monterrey, were playing away in Guadalajara.

'Juanita!' yelled her friends. 'Come, sit with us.'

Juanita waved and made her way over to them. 'Thank you for keeping the seat for me, *amigo*,' she said, sliding into the chair.

'Where is your police dog?' asked a grinning, toothless man. He leaned in close to be heard above the noise. 'Does he not support Monterrey?'

Juanita laughed. 'Toltec is not a big fan of football,' she shouted. 'He is back at the police kennels for the night. He prefers the sport of chasing criminals.'

Monterrey won the game, and once it was over the restaurant began to empty. But some, like the sergeant, stayed to celebrate the win. Laughing with friends, Juanita sensed someone standing behind her. Looking around, she saw a stranger at her right shoulder. The man was wearing a dark business suit and an open-necked shirt.

'You are Juanita Del Ray, head of the Monterrey Police Dog Unit?' the stranger asked in a cold, unfriendly tone.

Juanita nodded. 'Who wants to know?'

'You must come with us,' said another voice.

Looking to her left, Juanita saw a second man. He also wore a business suit, which was a rare sight in this restaurant. 'Who are you?' she demanded.

'We are from the office of the Ministry of Justice's Internal Investigations Unit,' said the first man. 'We need you to come down to the ministry to answer some questions.'

'Questions? What about?'

'Corruption,' said the first man.

'Corruption?' Juanita almost laughed. 'I am the most honest officer in the entire police force.'

This brought laughter from her friends at the table.

But the second man in a suit was not amused. 'Is that so? We have been watching you. Who paid for your meal tonight?'

Juanita shrugged. 'Me, but I have yet to pay for it.'

'Where is the bill?' asked the second man. 'There is no bill, because your friend the restaurant owner does not charge you, a serving police officer. Is that not correct?'

'I will pay for my meal when I leave.'

'So you say. Under the laws of this state, and of this country, the fact that the restaurant owner does not charge you constitutes bribery, Sergeant Del Ray,' said the first man, clapping a hand on Juanita's shoulder. 'Bribery and corruption.'

'Come on! I will pay. That is not enough for you to waste your time with me . . .'

The first man leaned in close. 'There is more,' he said in a low, conspiratorial voice. 'Much more for you to answer for. So, come quietly, answer some questions at the ministry and there need not be any cause for alarm. Then you can go home to your children.'

Juanita had heard of the shadowy Internal Investigations Unit, but its members wore plain clothes and kept a low profile. 'Show me your ID,' she demanded.

The first man produced a business card with 'Ministry of Justice' printed on it.

After inspecting it, Juanita nodded. 'Okay, I will come with you. But I assure you I am an honest cop. I have done nothing wrong.' She stood up. 'You are not going to handcuff me, are you?'

'That will not be necessary as long as you cooperate with us,' said the first man.

With each man on either side of her, Juanita was hustled out of the bar. From behind his counter, the restaurant owner watched the three of them leave. He frowned, not liking what he saw. Once they'd left, he called the police.

Outside, the trio walked along the street and around the corner to an alley. The light here was poor, with the scene dimly lit by a street lamp on the corner.

'We'll have your gun belt, Sergeant,' said the first man as they reached a dark-blue pick-up. The second man unlocked the doors.

Without a word, Juanita unbuckled the belt. It held a bunch of her equipment as well as a Heckler & Koch USP semi-automatic pistol. She handed it to the first man, who motioned for her to get in the back of the four-door pick-up. Juanita did as she was bidden, and the first man slid in beside her and closed the door. The second man got in behind the wheel and started the engine.

'Now, Sergeant Del Ray,' said the first man, jabbing her in the ribs with her own pistol, 'just stay calm and do as we say, and you will live to see your family again.'

'What . . . what's going on?' she stammered, suddenly fearful for her life.

'You'll find out soon enough,' said the second man. Reaching over from the driver's seat, he held out a length of dark cloth. 'Put this on, and do a good job of it.'

Juanita did as she was told and blindfolded herself. Then they drove off, joined a busy street and turned north. Juanita didn't know where they went after that, just as she had no inkling where she was being taken, or why.

CHAPTER 15

Sitting in an office at SAPD HQ, Ben looked at images on the computer screen in front of him. As Captain De Silva had promised, he'd arranged for the criminal intelligence section of the San Antonio Police Department to give Ben a briefing on the three crime cartels that used Monterrey as their base of operations – the Árbol, the Estrella and the smaller, newer Americana gang. They also gave him a USB containing all the information they had. This was mostly historical background data on the known members of each cartel and the crimes associated with them.

Ben's mind turned to Caesar. He wondered how his canine mate was doing. Ben hoped his abductors were looking after him properly and taking care what they gave him to eat and drink. The list of items that humans loved but were harmful to dogs – in some cases resulting in death – was long. That list ranged from alcohol, tea and coffee to chocolate, commercial cat food, peanuts, tomato leaves and stems, and any fatty foods. Who knew how much care the gang members would take with Caesar's diet?

Ben forced himself to focus on the data in front of him. He'd discovered that there was precious little up-to-date information on the cartel leaders. The identity of the Americana's current leader was unknown. Ben studied a picture of the boss of Estrella, Antonio Lopez, in his Marine Corps uniform. He was a handsome, businesslike man. Then there was Carlos Marron, also known as the Green Parrot. According to the SAPD briefing, Marron loved Elvis Presley and had not been seen in public in eight years – yet was known to live in Monterrey. Ben was looking at a blurry picture of the Green Parrot taken ten years ago, when Captain De Silva walked into the office.

'Marron made up his own nickname, you know,' said De Silva, as he stood at Ben's shoulder. 'I guess he thought it would make him sound a bit more romantic than plain "Charles Brown". Or, as my guys like to call him, Charlie Brown – just like the cartoon character in *Peanuts*. They think he's a bit of a joke with his Elvis hairstyle and all. Marron makes his men call him "*padrino*". It means "godfather". He's watched way too many Hollywood movies, that one.'

'He can't be that much of a joke,' Ben responded. 'He's managed to avoid being arrested all these years.'

'Yeah, well, that's only because the Mexican police are an even bigger joke than he is. And no one has dared to rat on Marron. Not since one of his former gang members agreed to testify against him in court. That guy disappeared without a trace. The rumour is that he was fed to the sharks off the Pacific coast by the Velásquez brothers, criminal associates of Marron in Baja California, and that members of the Federal Police were involved in his disappearance.'

'The Mexican police were involved?' Ben swung around on his swivel chair to face the captain. 'They protected the Green Parrot?'

'Partner, if you pay enough, you can buy anything in Mexico – including the cops. Marron bought them off. Back then, pay for Mexican cops was lousy, but it has since doubled.' De Silva shrugged. 'Even so, beat cops see the cartels making millions and want a piece of the action.'

'You don't have much time for the Mexican police?'

'I got zero time for the Mexican police. Those who ain't corrupt are just plain lazy.'

Ben ran a hand through his hair. 'But if Caesar is in Mexico, I'm going to need the help of the Mexican police to locate and extract him, Captain.'

De Silva nodded. 'I know, I know. I've got one reliable contact with the Federales in Monterrey. A lieutenant by the name of Pedro Peters. Somewhere back in his history he's got an American-born naval captain for an ancestor, which explains his last name. Peters should be able to help you.'

'Good,' said Ben, turning back to the screen. 'Marron is on the top of my list of suspects because he had good reason to kidnap Caesar. More reason, at least, than the bosses of Estrella or Americana. Maybe he wanted to use Caesar to protect himself from more bombs like the ones that were targeting his brother, Rocky.'

De Silva nodded thoughtfully. 'That makes sense.'

'I need to go down to Monterrey, Captain.'

De Silva let out a long sigh. 'It's dangerous.'

'I'm no stranger to danger. It's all part of my job in Special Forces.'

'Okay, soldier boy. Let me see what I can set up with the authorities in Mexico.' De Silva pronounced it 'Mehico', as Mexicans would. 'You don't want to go wandering around alone – you've got no authority down there in bandit territory. And I'll set up transport for you. But I'm not taking any responsibility for you once you cross that border. You got me, partner?'

'Copy that, Captain,' Ben responded. 'Just get me down there. I'll do the rest.'

Ben was on his way to the University of Texas accommodation when his mobile phone rang.

'Hi, it's Amanda,' said a familiar voice.

The worried look on Ben's face was replaced with a

smile. 'Amanda!' He had immediately recognised the voice of his good friend Amanda Ritchie, an Australian newspaper journalist who had helped him the last time Caesar had gone missing. 'How are you going?'

'I'm fine, thanks, Ben. Your mum just told me that Caesar was kidnapped in Texas. I'm really worried for you all. The kids must be so upset.'

A frown dented Ben's brow. 'My mother shouldn't have told you that. Caesar's disappearance is not for publication. It's classified information.'

'Hey, I'm not just any reporter,' Amanda replied, sounding offended. 'I thought we were friends. Your mother told me about Caesar in confidence, and of course I'll respect that confidence.'

'Sorry, Amanda, I'm under a lot of stress,' said Ben, feeling foolish. 'I know you'll keep it to yourself.'

'Maybe I can help.'

'I don't know how you could help at this point. We're still not entirely sure where Caesar is.'

'But you have an idea?' said Amanda. 'Mexico, right?'

'Could be. How'd you know? My mother again?'

Amanda laughed. 'No, I used my powers of deduction. Any connection with the car bombs in San Antonio last week?'

'There could be a connection, yes.'

'Do you think one of the crime cartels could have taken Caesar?'

Ben smiled again. Amanda had always impressed him with how quick she put two and two together. 'It's a possibility.'

'Okay. Well, keep me posted. I'll do whatever I can to help. I love Caesar too, you know.'

'Will do. Thanks, Amanda. I appreciate the offer. Caesar would, too, if he knew.'

After he hung up, Ben sat on the back seat of the cab as it sped along a San Antonio freeway, a faint smile lingering on his lips. He thought about how much Amanda, a feisty, independent woman, reminded him of his late wife, Marie. She also had the same kind heart as Marie. Twice, in Australia and Afghanistan, Amanda had been involved in his and Caesar's lives. How she could help them now, Ben could not imagine, but he was comforted by the offer.

🐾🐾

'Come, César, we are going to visit with someone who can understand a dog like you,' called Vargas. He traipsed over to the other side of the garage. When he reached Caesar, he let out a gasp. 'What have you done?'

Caesar came to his feet.

'You have pooped on the floor of El Loro's garage!'

Caesar couldn't help it. He had to relieve himself

somewhere, and Vargas had kept him chained up in the garage.

'You stupid, stupid dog!' Vargas raged, staring at the mess.

Caesar couldn't understand Spanish, but he understood perfectly well from Vargas's tone that he was in trouble. Backing away, he dropped his eyes to the floor.

'I thought you were well-trained,' Vargas growled as he fetched a spade. 'El Loro Verde would kill me if he found your poop right beside his Ferrari!'

Caesar watched him as Vargas scooped up the poop and dropped it in a rubbish bin.

'Come, poopy dog,' said Vargas. 'Come earn your keep.'

He unhitched Caesar's leash and led him from the garage via a side door. A black Volkswagen van stood waiting in the forecourt outside, its engine running. Vargas opened the rear doors and urged Caesar to jump inside. When the labrador hesitated, Vargas impatiently kicked him in the rump.

'Get in, poopy dog!' he yelled.

With a pained yelp, Caesar leapt into the van. Vargas let go of the leash and slammed the doors shut, then climbed into the cab beside the driver. The driver, an Árbol *pistolero*, had a pistol in his belt and a Heckler & Koch MP5 submachine gun under his seat.

'Go, go, go!' Vargas urged.

As the van edged forward, the gate clattered to one side. From an unseen control room, an Árbol guard was keeping watch. The van nosed onto the road, and the boys playing soccer immediately stopped what they were doing and respectfully stood back.

One of the boys, no more than ten years old, called out, 'Viva El Loro Verde!'

Vargas smiled and waved. 'That kid José is eager to work for El Loro,' he remarked to the driver. Vargas guessed that, before many years had passed, José would be running errands for Árbol on his first step to becoming one of their thousands of operatives. Another ten years from now, Vargas surmised, José would probably be killed in a shootout with rivals or the police, or spend the rest of his life serving time behind bars. There was a one-in-ten chance José would survive to make more money from crime than his hardworking labourer parents had seen in their lives.

The gate slid back to seal El Loro in his suburban fortress once more. That was the price he paid for his life of crime; he had become a prisoner in his own home.

🐾🐾

The van made its way across town to an abandoned factory in the east. As it passed through a roller door, Vargas spied Diego waiting for him. On the far side of the deserted building stood a dark-blue pick-up truck. Tommy was hauling Sergeant Juanita Del Ray from the back of it as the van pulled up alongside them.

'Take the blindfold off her,' Vargas commanded, climbing out of the van.

Tommy tugged at the piece of cloth circling the sergeant's head. Juanita squinted as her eyes readjusted to the light.

'Look at you in your police uniform,' said Vargas. 'This is no job for a woman.'

'You are *pistoleros*?' Juanita demanded, standing tall. 'If you intend to kill me, do it now. Tell my children that I died bravely.'

'Such dramatics!' Vargas returned with a laugh in his voice. 'We are not going to kill you. Not if you help us.'

'I do not help the cartels.' Juanita eyed them carefully. 'You are with one of the cartels, are you not?'

Vargas grinned. '*Amiga*, we are just employees of a dog-sitting service that is in need of your great skills with one of our four-legged friends.' This brought cackles of laughter from Diego and Tommy. Vargas walked to the van and opened the back doors. 'Out, poopy dog. Out!' he snarled.

In an instant, Caesar launched himself at the man. Vargas had made the mistake of failing to secure Caesar's leash to the van's interior. With an alarmed cry, Vargas staggered backwards while Caesar bounded away, intent on escaping his captors.

'Mother Maria!' exclaimed Vargas. 'Infernal, dog-pooping devil! Get that dog, you idiots! He cannot get away!' Diego and Tommy both set off at the run in pursuit of the labrador, but Vargas called one of them back. 'No, not you, Tommy. You keep an eye on the cop!' He turned to the VW driver, who was still behind the wheel. 'Rodriguez! Cut the dog off with the van.'

With a squeal of rubber on concrete, Rodriguez drove the van to a ramp on the left that Caesar was heading for. He slew to a halt and blocked it with the vehicle. Jumping out, he stood ready to intercept the dog. Seeing the man up ahead standing in his path, Caesar darted right to avoid Rodriguez. Diego, running behind him, lunged for the leash trailing behind the labrador. He sprawled across the factory floor, missing the leash by centimetres.

'You idiot!' cried Vargas, running up to him and panting hard. 'Get him! Get him!'

Grimacing, Diego pulled himself to his feet to set off after Caesar. From the other end of the factory, Tommy watched the chase unfold. With a Glock pistol in one hand, he had pushed Juanita up against the side of the pick-up.

'You could not catch a cold if you tried, Diego!' Tommy yelled derisively. Shaking his head, he raised his Glock and took aim as Caesar searched for a new escape route. Closing one eye, Tommy squinted along the barrel. Shifting his aim to be slightly ahead of the running dog, he fired. The gun coughed, and a bullet chipped into the concrete floor immediately in front of the labrador, sending dust and concrete chips flying up into Caesar's face. Caesar leapt away to the left.

'Tommy, what are you doing?' called Vargas. He came to a halt, puffing hard. He put his hands on his hips and bent double as he tried to catch his breath. 'You cannot shoot the dog. El Loro will shoot *you* if you harm it!'

'I am not shooting the dog,' Tommy returned. 'I am too good a shot to miss. I am trying to make the dog stop.' He squeezed off another round, which flew past Caesar and ploughed into the end wall. 'Fool of a dog!'

Caesar stopped at a large rectangular opening in the floor. A goods lift the size of a suburban garage had once stood there. Glancing around, Caesar saw Diego bearing down on him. Tommy fired at him a third time. Another bullet chipped the floor, this time beside Caesar. Instinctively, the labrador reeled back.

Just as Diego was making another dive for his leash, Caesar leapt into the yawning chasm in front of him. Diego's hand grabbed for the end of the leash, but it slipped through his fingers. Caesar fell the long distance to the floor below and landed awkwardly on his side.

Vargas reached the opening, panting. He looked down anxiously at Caesar lying still on the floor below. 'You idiots!' Vargas raged. 'If that dog is dead, you are dead! Tommy, bring the cop. She knows about dogs.'

The men ran down the fire stairs and clustered around Caesar. Sergeant Del Ray knelt beside him, carefully feeling his body for broken bones.

'Is the dog dead?' asked Rodriguez.

'He's alive,' said Juanita. 'I think he was winded by the fall. And his ribs . . .' As she spoke, Caesar turned his head and growled at her. 'Now, now, César,' she said soothingly, 'Juanita will not harm you.' She looked up at Vargas. 'Here, he is sore.' She indicated the labrador's side. 'Perhaps broken ribs. Perhaps they are only bruised. It was a brave thing he did, jumping from such a height.'

'A stupid thing, if you ask me,' Tommy remarked.

'You must make César well,' Vargas commanded.

'Is *this* why you abducted me?' said Juanita. 'What is so special about this dog?'

'The American television says that he is the best exploding dog in the world,' Vargas replied. 'You and César will protect our boss from bombs.'

Juanita had overheard Vargas mention the name of El Loro Verde, and had deduced that her abductors were from the Árbol crime cartel. 'You need a handler for this dog?' she said. It occurred to her that as long as the dog was useful to these thugs, her safety was guaranteed.

'You will look after the dog,' said Vargas, 'and you will tell us when the dog sniffs a bomb.'

'Okay, I understand,' she replied, stroking Caesar's head. Her own dog, Toltec, was a Belgian malinois trained to sniff out illegal drugs. She had no experience with the detection of explosives and she had no idea what Caesar's 'signature' might be. Toltec, like all police and military sniffer dogs, had his own signature for indicating that he had located contraband. It was possible that she would recognise Caesar's signature, but it was just as likely that she wouldn't. To stay alive, Juanita decided she would have to pretend to these Árbol cretins that she knew exactly what she was doing until an opportunity to escape came along.

'You can read this dog?' said Diego. 'You will know when he smells a bomb?'

'Of course,' Juanita lied. 'Am I not an expert with sniffer dogs? Am I not the *chief* of the Police Dog Unit? I am the best dog handler in all of Mexico!' She hoped her bravado worked and that they wouldn't ask her to do a bomb-sniffing demonstration with this foreign labrador. 'But for the moment, this dog needs rest. That fall could have killed him.' She looked up at the gaping hole through which Caesar had fallen. 'Such a long drop.'

'All right,' said Vargas, sounding relieved.

'What do we do with them now?' Diego asked.

'We take them back to the house,' replied Vargas. 'Near El Loro Verde.'

'You sure about that?' Tommy queried. 'A cop under *el padrino's* roof? Shouldn't we keep them someplace else? At one of our safe houses, maybe.'

'How can they protect *el padrino* from bombs when they're halfway across town?' Vargas shook his head. 'Idiot! They must be where he is at all times. Blindfold the cop. We're going back to the house; all of us.'

CHAPTER 16

In dawn's early light, a small Mexican Army MD 500 Defender helicopter eased down onto the helipad on the roof of the Monterrey Police Headquarters. The chopper's right side door opened and, after thanking the crew for the ride from San Antonio, Ben Fulton climbed out lugging his kitbag. Bending low beneath the heelo's spinning rotors, Ben ran to a Federal Police lieutenant waiting alone at the rooftop door. Behind him, the helicopter took to the sky again.

'Welcome to Mexico, Sergeant Fulton,' said the lieutenant, shaking Ben by the hand and smiling. 'I'm Pedro Peters.' Of average height, he had blond hair and blue eyes. His cheeks dimpled when he smiled and he spoke English with only the faintest of foreign accents, as if he had spent time in America.

Ben smiled in return. 'Captain De Silva of the SAPD said that you might be able to help me find my EDD, sir. I'm working on a hunch that he's been brought here.'

'You never know,' said Peters, guiding Ben through

the door and down a flight of stairs. 'We had a development overnight that could suggest that your EDD is indeed here in Monterrey.'

'Really?' Ben responded with a mixture of surprise and delight. 'What kind of development, sir?'

'The head of Monterrey's dog squad, Sergeant Juanita Del Ray, was taken from a local restaurant last night. Her abductors posed as officers from the Ministry of Justice.'

'And the Ministry of Justice has confirmed that they are not holding the sergeant?'

Lieutenant Peters nodded. 'The restaurant's owner was suspicious. He rang the police after Sergeant Del Ray was taken away. Unfortunately, it was too late to trace her and her abductors.'

He led the way through a fire escape to a floor filled with desks. Some, even at this early hour, were occupied by police officers. It struck Ben how few of these desks were equipped with computers. Back in Texas, every single desk in the San Antonio Police Department had a computer on it, and every possible electronic aid was available to the San Antonio Police. Here, the Monterrey Police looked like they were fighting crime on a shoestring budget.

'So, have the bad guys made a ransom demand for the release of Sergeant Del Ray?' he asked.

'No,' Peters replied, 'and, if you ask me, Sergeant Fulton, there will be no ransom demand for Juanita.

The question we have all been asking ourselves is this: What does a crime cartel want with a police dog handler? My colleagues have come up with a variety of possible motives, some of them not pleasant to think about. On the other hand, they may just want her talents as a dog handler. Logical, huh?'

'Very,' Ben agreed.

'More than that, they need Juanita to handle a particular dog. Maybe a bomb-sniffing dog that has just been kidnapped across the border in Texas by the very same *pistoleros*. What do you think?'

Ben nodded. 'It adds up, Lieutenant.' He didn't want to get his hopes up in case this all turned out to be a red herring. If Caesar wasn't here in Mexico, Ben had no idea where else to look for him. Such a scenario didn't even bear thinking about. As far as Ben was concerned, this lead had to be genuine.

On his computer screen Lieutenant Peters brought up a group photo of Juanita Del Ray with her sniffer dog, Toltec, and the rest of the dogs and handlers of the Monterrey Police Dog Unit. 'That's Juanita,' he said, pointing to her in the picture.

Ben studied the photograph. 'If she and Caesar are being held together,' he mused, 'at least Caesar will have some company from someone who knows dogs.'

He would take comfort from that.

Gingerly, Caesar came to his feet. His leather collar had been returned to his neck and, once again, his leash trailed from it. Though his ribs had been bruised when he dropped through the floor of the deserted factory, none were broken. Since returning to the Green Parrot's mansion, Caesar and Sergeant Del Ray were being kept prisoner in a shed in the property's small backyard.

'Are you okay now, César?' Juanita asked, reaching out and patting his head.

Caesar's tail began to wag. Not only did Caesar possess a phenomenal sense of smell, he could sense that, unlike the others, Juanita was kind and could be trusted. It was true that Caesar could pick up traces of explosive chemical on the likes of Vargas, Diego and Tommy, from the weapons they carried. But Ben and Charlie and the other soldiers that Caesar worked with in the Australian Army and GRRR routinely carried weapons and explosives, yet Caesar knew they were the good guys. And it wasn't simply that Vargas and the others smelled different as a result of their Mexican diet, because Sergeant Del Ray had a similar diet to the gangsters. Caesar could nevertheless sense that she was one of the good guys. With his tail still wagging, he nestled in beside her.

Juanita pulled his head in close and gave him a gentle cuddle, knowing how sore he must be after his tumble. 'We are prisoners together, you and I,' she said. 'You made a heroic attempt to escape, my friend.' She lowered her voice. 'And we will succeed in escaping from these people, you and I both. Just you wait and see.'

Suddenly, there came a scratching sound from one side of the wooden shed. Caesar heard it first. His ears pricked up and he pulled back from Juanita.

'What is it?' Juanita whispered to Caesar. 'Do you hear something?'

Caesar cocked his head to one side. There was the scratching noise again. Lowering his head, he followed the noise to the wall. As the scratching continued, Caesar let out a little whimper, then began to paw at the earth floor. Soon, he was dragging dirt away from the bottom of the wall.

Digging was a habit that Ben had attempted to train out of Caesar from a young age. Not only did Nan Fulton like her rosebushes left alone, Caesar's digging habit could pose a danger to Ben and himself while on operations. An explosive detection dog could accidentally set off explosives he was trying to dig up. Caesar's job was just to locate explosives, leaving bomb-disposal experts to do the rest. But Caesar had never entirely lost the digging habit, and it had helped him to get out of trouble several times in the past. Once more, he yielded to the temptation to dig with his big webbed feet.

'César, what are you doing?' Juanita whispered, crawling to join him. 'Are you trying to escape?'

Caesar paused and glanced around at Juanita with a look that was all concentration, then resumed his digging. Before long, he had created a small hole beneath the wall. From outside, a miniature dog snout poked through. It belonged to Rosa, Lola's pink chihuahua. Withdrawing her head, Rosa gave a yap. It was as if she were trying to encourage Caesar to escape through the hole. The labrador redoubled his efforts. Twice he stopped to try to push his head out through the hole, but each time he found the hole wasn't big enough.

Finally, the gap was sufficiently large for him to fit his head through. Pulling with his front legs and pushing with his back legs, Caesar was able to wriggle his way beneath the wall and scramble out into the yard beyond.

'Bravo, César!' Juanita whispered as she watched his tail disappear through the hole.

Outside, in the long, narrow, weed-infested yard which ran the width of the house, Rosa stood waiting for the big labrador. Excited that she had a playmate, the little pink dog began to run around, yapping. But as much as Caesar loved to play, he wasn't like most other dogs. He was a highly trained war dog, and he spent more time with soldiers than with dogs. He was missing one soldier in particular – Sergeant Ben Fulton – and was determined to locate him. Caesar shook the dirt from his coat then, looking around in the morning sunlight, he spotted a wooden fence hemming in the rear of the yard.

Trotting to the fence, Caesar gazed up at the top with a thoughtful look on his face. In his mind, Caesar calculated that, if he took a running jump at it, he could reach the top of the fence, clear it and make good his escape. Behind him, Rosa continued to yap, trying to coax him into chasing her. But Caesar's thoughts went to Juanita. He turned and bounded back to the shed. He could see that Juanita was trying to enlarge the hole from inside the shed, to make it big enough for her own escape. Barking his encouragement to Juanita, he began to dig from his side. As he dug, little Rosa ran around him, continuing to yap.

All this barking eventually attracted Lola's attention. Hearing the racket, she opened a window and leaned out to see what was going on in the yard. 'Rosa! What is all the noise about?' she demanded. And then she saw Caesar digging furiously beside the shed. 'Vargas! Vargas!' she called with alarm. 'Your sniffing dog is escaping!'

Less than a minute later Vargas, Diego and Tommy came rushing into the yard from the house. Caesar momentarily stopped digging and turned to see the gangsters before he resumed digging in an attempt to free his new friend Juanita Del Ray.

'Got you, poopy dog!' Vargas declared victoriously, grabbing Caesar's leash.

Caesar bared his teeth and growled at Vargas.

'Don't you growl at me, poopy dog!' Vargas snarled, prodding Caesar's bruised ribs with his foot.

This brought a pained yelp from Caesar.

Tommy knelt down on one knee and surveyed the hole beside the shed. 'Looks like the dog was trying to dig the cop out, Vargas.'

'Neither of them is going any place,' said Vargas, yanking the leash and pulling Caesar closer.

'Aren't you afraid the dog will bite you, Vargas?' said Diego. 'It looks pretty mean to me.'

'He wouldn't dare bite me!' Vargas returned. Gripping the leash tighter with one hand, he removed a SIG Sauer semi-automatic pistol from his belt with his other hand and pointed it at Caesar.

Caesar glared up at him but made no more sounds and did not move. Rosa, meantime, dashed in and fastened her tiny jaws around Vargas's right ankle.

Letting out an alarmed howl, Vargas kicked his leg around, trying to force the dog to let go. 'Get off! Get off!' he bellowed.

As Rosa hung on like a limpet, Diego and Tommy roared with laughter at the sight until Vargas finally shook the chihuahua from his ankle. The little dog went rolling across the yard. When she got back on her feet, she yapped defiantly at Vargas from what she thought would be a safe distance.

'Idiot of a dog!' Vargas raged, turning his weapon on the pink ball of fluff.

'Vargas!' yelled Lola from the window above. 'Don't you dare harm a hair of my little Rosa's body!'

'The rat dog does not have hair, it has fur,' he corrected her, lowering his pistol.

'*You* will not have hair in a minute,' Lola fumed. 'I will tell my husband to have every hair plucked from your body if you hurt my Rosa.'

'Take it easy,' said Vargas. 'I will not harm the rat dog as long as you keep it away from me.' He returned his attention to Caesar. 'As for you, poopy dog, we will have to find a better place to keep you and the cop.'

'Put them in the laundry,' Lola called. 'It has bars on the window and is never used anyway.'

Vargas turned to Diego and Tommy. 'You two, bring the cop to the laundry.'

With that, Vargas led Caesar toward his latest prison, in the heavily guarded mansion of the Green Parrot.

CHAPTER 17

In the busy cantina at Monterrey Police Headquarters, Ben was eating a hearty breakfast of bacon and eggs with Lieutenant Peters when he was interrupted by a call from Amanda Ritchie.

'Don't you ever sleep, Amanda?' Ben said good-naturedly.

'Plenty of time for sleeping on my flight to the States,' Amanda replied.

This caught Ben by surprise. 'You're travelling to the US? Where are you now?'

'I'm at Sydney Airport, waiting for my flight to Dallas. Then I'm coming to wherever you are. I've convinced my editor there's a big story for me to cover over there.'

Ben frowned. 'You didn't reveal that Caesar had been abducted, did you?'

'No, I promised I wouldn't, didn't I! I told my boss I was working on confidential information. He knows from my track record to trust me when I say there's a big story in the wind, even if I can't reveal what it's about straight-away. So, where are you, Ben? Still in San Antonio, or are you now in Monterrey?'

Ben was surprised. 'Why do you think I'd be in Monterrey?'

'Rocky Marron was from Monterrey.'

Ben smiled. 'You've done your homework.'

'That's my job, Sergeant Fulton,' she said teasingly. 'I thought you might be in Monterrey, so I booked a room at the Hilton Garden Inn there.'

'Monterrey is a dangerous place, Amanda,' Ben warned.

'My job has taken me to plenty of dangerous places. You know that, Ben. I'm used to it. Anyway, they're calling my flight – I'll see you soon.'

'Okay. Bye.' Smiling to himself, Ben hung up.

'Good news?' asked Lieutenant Peters.

'I'm not sure,' Ben confessed, though he couldn't deny that he was looking forward to seeing his friend. 'So, where do we go from here?' he asked the lieutenant. 'How do we track down Caesar and your missing sergeant?'

Lieutenant Peters took a sip of his coffee. 'First, we find the Green Parrot.'

'Great! What are we waiting for?'

'This is not so easy. We believe that he lives somewhere in Monterrey, but this is a big city, of several million people. It is easy to disappear here. And none of the few people who do know where the Green Parrot is hiding out is brave enough – or foolish enough – to reveal precisely where.'

'Okay. But you must have some idea of where he is.'

'We have heard on the streets that his house is a mansion. So, we think he must live in one of the rich suburbs in the south of the city, pretending to be a legitimate businessman. That is all. We need a break, Ben. We need someone to spill the beans and tell us where to find the Green Parrot.'

Ben nodded as he appreciated the problem. 'You have your ear to the ground out there in the city?'

'Naturally. We have paid informants. The crazy thing is that people here talk about Marron all the time on social media: "El Loro Verde does this for the poor", "El Loro Verde did that to make the police look foolish". They will even say that they had bumped into him at this bar or that restaurant. We never know how much of that sort of boasting is true – if any.'

'Do you trust what you see on the internet?'

'Personally, I don't believe a great deal of what I read on there. To me, the internet is the tool of liars, braggarts and fools. But I'd believe it if someone tweeted they'd seen the Green Parrot at an Elvis tribute performance.'

Ben nodded. 'I've heard he's a big Elvis fan.'

'The world's biggest, by all accounts,' said Lieutenant Peters. He was about to say something when his phone rang. He glanced at the screen and sighed. 'Excuse me.'

Peters spoke urgently in Spanish for a few moments, then hung up.

'Good news, Ben,' he announced with a smile. 'It looks like my boys have identified the two *pistoleros* who kidnapped Sergeant Del Ray as the same guys who took your dog in San Antonio. Come to my office and take a look.'

'The weekly package has arrived from the Velásquez brothers, *Padrino*,' Vargas announced, walking into the living room. That package was filled with cash, from Árbol criminal activities.

An old Elvis Presley movie, *G.I. Blues*, was playing on one of the screens. 'I have seen this movie a hundred times before,' said Carlos Marron, not taking his eyes off the movie, 'but every time I see something new. Look at the jeep in the background there.' He pointed to the screen. 'The registration plate begins with "EP". A clever touch from the producers, don't you think?'

'Fascinating,' Vargas replied. He was not an Elvis fan. 'What do you want me to do with the package?'

'You allowed a package into the house?' Marron sat up and switched off the movie. 'Estrella could have planted a bomb in the package, you idiot! We could all be blown sky-high! Where is it now?'

Vargas paled. 'It's, er, in the garage, *Padrino*.'

'Get the sniffer dog to check it out. That's what it is here for. Now, Vargas! *Rápido! Rápido!*'

'*Sí, Padrino*.'

Vargas hurried away, summoning Diego and Tommy to follow him. The three of them went to the laundry, where they found Juanita sitting on the tiled floor with Caesar lying at her feet.

'You, bring the dog,' Vargas snapped, pointing to Juanita.

The sergeant rose to her feet and took up Caesar's leash. 'Come, my friend,' she said to the labrador. 'Let's see what they want.'

Caesar trusted Juanita and accompanied her without resistance.

The three thugs took dog and handler down to the garage. 'Check out that package over there,' Vargas commanded, pointing to a box sitting in front of one of the garage doors. 'You have ten minutes to tell us whether it is okay or not.'

He, Diego and Tommy then retreated to the floor above.

Juanita led Caesar to the box, stopping about three metres away from it. 'What do you think, César?' Juanita asked her canine companion. She pointed to the box, its openings covered with grey duct tape.

Caesar looked up at her with an expression that seemed to say, *What's that, new friend? What do you want me to do?*

'Is there an explosive device in there, César? Is it an IED?'

Still Caesar didn't know what she wanted him to do. If he had been working with Ben, he would have received a familiar command: 'Seek on, Caesar.' Upon hearing this, he would have immediately gone into explosive-detecting mode. But Juanita didn't know this.

A bemused Caesar looked up at her, his head tilted to one side. The expression on his face seemed to say, *I don't know what you want me to do.*

'Come, let us take a closer look,' said Juanita, hiding her fear that the box might explode at any moment. If she was to keep the gangsters happy, she had to do her best to sort this out, hopefully with Caesar's help. The pair moved to stand right in front of the box. Juanita dropped to one knee beside Caesar and gently tapped the top of the box. 'What do you smell, César? Can you smell explosives in here?'

Caesar lowered his head to the cardboard and then, turning to look at her, sat down.

Juanita grimaced. 'Is that your signature?'

But Caesar seemed more interested in her than in the box, and that didn't fit with what Juanita knew about sniffer dogs. When Toltec detected contraband, he became very excited and wouldn't take his eyes off the object. Caesar seemed disinterested in the box, which Juanita deduced to mean explosives were not present. She proceeded to strip the duct tape from the top of the box, piece by piece, until she was able to pull back the top flaps. In front of her lay stack upon stack of one-hundred dollar bills. There had to be tens of thousands of dollars in that box.

Vargas and his cronies appeared behind her. 'No need for you to worry about all that, lady.' Grabbing her arm, he roughly hauled her to her feet and away from the box.

Caesar turned to Vargas, baring his teeth.

Vargas pulled the SIG Sauer pistol from his belt and pointed it at the labrador. 'Do not growl at me, César!' he said menacingly. 'Not if you know what is good for you.'

🐾🐾

Lieutenant Peters turned the folder that lay open on his desk so Ben was able to see the two mug shots. 'My boys think they have a match. The SAPD sent us the description that Cindy Levine gave of the two men who stole your Caesar. We matched it to the description that the owner of the restaurant gave of the two men who kidnapped Sergeant Del Ray. Both are convicted Árbol *pistoleros* who escaped in a mass breakout from Apodaca Prison that Árbol staged a few years back.'

Ben studied the photographs, lodging the images in his memory for future reference. 'What are their names?'

'The man on the left is Diego Garcia. The other is Tomas el Uno, also known as Tommy the One.'

'Any idea where they are?'

'That, my friend, is not so easy to know. Like the Green Parrot, you can't just look these guys up in the phone book. But at least we know who we are looking for now.'

Sitting on his bed in the early hours of the morning, Ben Skyped his family.

'Have you got Caesar back yet?' Maddie asked anxiously. She, Josh and Nan sat on the living-room sofa.

'Not yet, sweetheart,' Ben replied wearily.

'You look tired, Ben,' Nan remarked. 'Are you getting enough sleep?'

Ben smiled. 'Yes, Mum. How's the drumming going, Josh? Keeping up the practice?'

'I've been too busy searching for clues about Caesar. There's nothing on the net about him being kidnapped. I've searched and searched. I thought I might be able to find something to help, like I did before.'

Josh had certainly been a help to his father in the past. He was the one who had identified where the Secretary-General of the UN was being held hostage in Afghanistan.

'We've kept his abduction a classified military secret for now,' explained Ben. 'We don't want anything about it to get out.'

'Why?' asked Josh, puzzled.

'We didn't want the media crawling all over the story. That would only complicate matters. News reports could tip off the bad guys about what we know and what we're thinking.'

'Oh,' said Josh. 'I suppose you're right.'

'What *do* you know, and what *are* you thinking, Ben?' asked Nan.

'We know who took Caesar, and we think we know, roughly, where he is.'

'That's great!' exclaimed Maddie. 'Just tell those hobble people to give Caesar back!'

'It's not that simple, Maddie,' Ben responded with a sigh. 'But we're working on it. By the way, I'll be seeing Amanda over here in the next day or so.'

'I like Amanda,' said Nan.

'She's nice,' said Josh.

'Say hello from us,' Nan added.

Ben nodded. 'I will.'

'Keep up the good work, Ben,' Nan said encouragingly. 'We know you'll get Caesar back.'

'Hopefully sooner rather than later,' said Ben. 'All of you keep your fingers crossed that we get a firm lead on Caesar's whereabouts.'

'We will, Daddy,' Maddie responded, holding up her crossed fingers for her father to see.

The next day after school, the familiar sound of Josh's drumming practice filled the house. Nan smiled to herself and set about preparing dinner. Maddie was sitting at the kitchen table doodling absently on a piece of paper. She seemed unusually introspective.

'You're particularly quiet today, Maddie,' said Nan. 'Are you worrying about Caesar?'

'I always worry about Caesar when he and Daddy are away,' Maddie replied. 'But Daddy said he would bring him home, so I know he will.'

'Anything else on your mind?'

Maddie shrugged. 'Harriet Blaze is getting a new mummy.'

'Is she?' Nan raised an eyebrow. 'How?'

'Her daddy is getting married again.'

'Ah. I see.'

'She said I would get a new mummy one day, too.'

Nan chuckled. 'Really? What made her say that?'

'She was being nasty, I think, after I didn't take Caesar to her birthday party.'

'Ah. Girls can be nasty like that sometimes. Don't let her worry you.'

'I don't need a new mummy,' Maddie said firmly. 'I've already got a mummy.'

Nan wondered if she was talking about her. 'You mean me?'

Maddie giggled. 'No, you're my nan. I mean my mummy.'

'Ah. Of course.'

It had been several years now since the children's mother, Marie Fulton, had passed away from breast cancer. Maddie had been quite young at the time of her death and didn't refer to her often.

'Why would I get a new mummy?' Maddie asked.

'Well, sometimes a daddy will marry again after his wife passes away,' Nan explained. 'But your dad is much too busy and away on missions too often to even think about something like that.'

'Yes, he is,' said Maddie, screwing up the piece of paper. 'And I don't want a new mummy!'

CHAPTER 18

Ben walked through the doors of the Hilton Garden Inn's coffee shop feeling a little apprehensive as well as pleased to be able to catch up with Amanda. A day had passed since they'd spoken on the phone. As glad as he would be to see her, he worried that this was a dangerous place for a journalist, let alone a female journalist. Here, Ben's Australian military fatigues didn't turn a single head. There were thousands of Mexican soldiers, sailors and airmen stationed in Monterrey as part of the government's bid to put an end to the crime wave in Nuevo León, and they were a regular sight all over the city.

'It's good to see you,' said Ben, bending to give Amanda a kiss on the cheek before sliding into the booth across from her. As he did, he recalled the very first time he met her – in a coffee shop back in Sydney, after Caesar had gone missing in Afghanistan.

'You must be worried sick,' said Amanda, reaching across the table and squeezing his arm. 'All this time, and no word of him.'

'We do have a lead,' said Ben, trying to sound upbeat.

'You do? Do you know where the Green Parrot is?' Amanda had lowered her voice so that hotel guests at adjoining tables couldn't overhear.

Ben shook his head. 'We are pretty certain that it was two of his gunmen who kidnapped Caesar. The same guys also nabbed a police dog handler here in Monterrey.'

Amanda raised her eyebrows. 'Really? To look after Caesar?'

'That's what I'm hoping.'

'So you haven't pinpointed the Green Parrot's location?'

'Not yet. He could be anywhere in this city.'

'What if I could get you that information?'

Ben looked at her with surprise. 'How could you manage that?'

Amanda smiled coyly. 'Well, I've noticed that there's a lot of chat on the internet about the Green Parrot – on one site in particular: Friends of the People. It tries to portray Carlos Marron like General Santa Anna and Pancho Villa and a lot of other historical revolutionaries from Mexican history – as a friend of the common people.'

Ben shook his head. 'Those men were dictators and bandits.'

'*We* know that, but a lot of Mexicans harbour romantic notions about those guys.' Amanda shrugged and opened her hands. 'What can I say? Poor people seem to need heroes. Anyway, I wrote an article on the flight over about how the rest of the world views the war between the crime cartels and the Mexican Government. In the article I mentioned how much I'd love to interview the Green Parrot in person, to get his perspective on the crime war. I mean, who else in the media is going to give him that sort of opportunity to put his own case forward? The plan entails submitting the article to the Friends of the People, with the hope that the Green Parrot will invite me to interview him.'

'That's a dangerous thing to contemplate,' said Ben, looking concerned. 'I wouldn't want you to put yourself at risk like that, even if it is for Caesar's sake.'

'Too late,' Amanda said with an impish grin. 'I've already sent them the article, and they've posted it on their site. Look.' Amanda pulled her iPad from her bag and showed Ben the site.

'It's in Spanish,' he said. 'Did you write it in Spanish or did they translate it?'

'I wrote it in Spanish. My mother's from Spain and she's multilingual. I was fluent in Spanish, French and Italian before I was ten years old.'

Ben tilted his head and smiled at Amanda. 'I didn't know that about you.'

Amanda grinned. 'There's a lot you don't know about

me, Ben. Anyway, my language skills have really helped me over the years in my job.'

'I bet they have,' said Ben. 'So, you're hoping the Green Parrot will set up an interview with you as a result of your article?'

Amanda nodded. 'From what I've heard, this Parrot guy has a big ego. If I play my cards right I might be able to get some clues about where's he's hiding out.'

Ben pulled a face. 'Sounds risky.'

'Well, I'll decide what to do when the time comes.'

Ben smiled, and shook his head. Amanda was being her typical feisty and independent self.

The concierge approached their table and held out a folded slip of paper to Amanda. 'A message was left for you, Miss Ritchie,' he advised.

'Who left the message?' Amanda demanded.

'I don't know,' the concierge replied. 'I was not at my desk when the message came.' Turning on his heel, he hurried away.

'What's it say?' Ben asked as Amanda read the message.

'It says: "El Loro Verde agrees to a Skype interview with you." They've provided a local phone number, too.'

'That was quick. Your article hasn't even been up for that long.' Ben suddenly grew serious. 'Please be careful, Amanda. It could be a hoax.'

'Well, even if it's for real,' Amanda said, taking out her phone, 'I'm not accepting the invitation. I don't want to Skype the Green Parrot. That's no good to us. I've got to be in the same room as him if I'm to pinpoint his location, and therefore Caesar's location, for you.' She dialled the number on the note.

'*Sí?*' a voice answered abruptly.

'This is Amanda Ritchie, the Australian journalist.'

'*Sí.*'

'I will only interview the Green Parrot if we are in the same room, face-to-face, or it's not on. Do you understand?'

'*Sí.*'

'Will you pass on the message?'

'*Sí.*' The call was then disconnected.

'Well?' Ben said expectantly.

Amanda put her phone away and looked him in the eye. 'Now, we wait.'

In the early hours of the next morning, Amanda was woken by the hotel phone.

'Yes? Who is this?' she answered groggily.

'Miss Ritchie, this is hotel reception,' came a young male voice. 'Please do not be alarmed, but there is a fire emergency on your floor of the hotel and the fire alarm is not working. Please leave your room immediately and wait for a staff member in the corridor. They will escort you from the hotel via the fire escape. Please hurry. Thank you.'

Amanda quickly jumped out of bed and pulled on the clothes she had been wearing the previous day. She slipped on her shoes, grabbed her bag and stepped out into the corridor. Immediately, an arm snaked around her neck. A rough hand clasped firmly over her mouth, preventing her from screaming, and something cold jabbed into her neck. After an instant's uncertainty, she realised it was the barrel of a gun. And suddenly she was very afraid.

'Say nothing,' came the soft, menacing voice of Tommy el Uno in her ear.

Amanda was hustled to the fire escape, where Diego was waiting for them. Like Tommy, Diego was wearing a ski mask, which covered his head and only revealed his dark eyes and solemn mouth. As Tommy tied a blindfold around her head, Diego quickly searched Amanda's bag and then frisked her, looking for a weapon, a hidden radio transmitter or a tracking device.

When Diego found none of these, the two men led Amanda all the way down to the hotel car park. Their hurried steps echoed around the concrete stairwell as they went. In the car park, the blindfolded Amanda found herself thrust into the back of a van.

'Keep quiet, and everything will be okay,' Tommy whispered in her ear.

'Where are you taking me?' she demanded.

'To see *el padrino*. Now, keep quiet!' He closed the van's rear doors, and the engine started.

Amanda slumped against the van's metal wall as it drove out of the car park and through the city for what she calculated to be ten minutes. As the van rolled along, Amanda took her mind back to the call she had received, the call that had sent her scurrying from her hotel room and into the arms of the bad guys. She kicked herself for falling into such an obvious trap.

Amanda had been in a similar situation once before in Lebanon. Hotel management had called her in the middle of the night, urging her to get out of the building because of a bomb threat they had received. That time the call had been legitimate, and she now remembered hearing the phone ring in the room next door to hers, as hotel management passed the same warning onto others. She had not heard the phone ring in the adjoining rooms this time. Amanda hoped she was genuinely being taken to a face-to-face interview with the Green Parrot and that she'd be set free again. She knew what big business the kidnap-and-ransom industry was for Mexican cartels. There was no guarantee that the promise of an interview wasn't merely a means of luring her into a trap, with the crooks intending to ransom her rather than let her interview their boss.

The van stopped for a minute, then eased forward. Amanda suspected they had just gone through a gate of some sort. The rattling of what sounded like a metal roller door could be heard before the van made its way down a slope. Soon after it came to a stop, the van's rear doors were flung open. Tommy and Diego reached in and hauled her out.

'Is this her?' asked a male voice.

'*Sí*, this is the Australian journalist,' Tommy replied. 'The telephone trick worked like a charm. It got her out of her room in a flash.'

'Have you frisked her?'

'Of course,' Diego responded indignantly. 'Do you think I'm an idiot?'

'What about for a bomb?' Vargas demanded.

'A bomb?' Diego snorted. 'Where would she have a bomb?'

'Did you check her shoes?' Vargas pointed to Amanda's sneakers. 'Terrorists have been known to hide plastic explosives in shoes. What if Estrella set us up? They organised two car bombs for Rocky, didn't they? So, we can't put anything past them.'

Neither Diego nor Tommy had an answer for that. Vargas, for all his frequent and annoying stupidity, was right. After what the Estrella cartel did in San Antonio, they could be expected to stop at nothing to get their boss.

'Diego, get the dog and the cop,' Vargas instructed.

Diego hurried away and collected Caesar and Juanita from their temporary prison in the laundry. Juanita led Caesar on a short leash, fearful of what was in store for them this time but keeping up a brave face. Caesar's tail was hanging limp, and every now and then he glanced up at her uncertainly.

When they reached the garage, Vargas called, 'You and the poopy dog, do your thing. Check this *señorita* for a bomb. Pay particular attention to her shoes.'

As soon as Caesar saw Amanda, his tail began to wag furiously. He knew Amanda well and recognised her as a good friend of Ben's. The sight of her suggested to him that Ben could not be far away. Excited, he pulled hard toward her and let out a bark.

'Is that you, Cae–?' Amanda began. She caught herself just in time. If she let it be known that she and Caesar knew each other, the game was up. 'Is that your idea of a welcome?' she said, correcting herself. 'Unleashing a dog on me.'

'He will not hurt you,' Tommy answered.

Juanita was surprised by Caesar's reaction. 'He seems to like her,' she said, as she led the labrador up to Amanda. When Caesar reared up on his back legs and tried to lick Amanda's face in greeting, Juanita tugged hard on the leash to pull him back.

'She is Australian and so is the dog,' said Vargas. 'Maybe he smells something familiar.'

Tommy chuckled. 'Does she smell like a kangaroo?'

Diego laughed.

'Make him check out her shoes, cop lady,' Vargas commanded.

Juanita dropped to one knee in front of Amanda and pulled Caesar in close. 'César, are there any explosives here? Huh?' She patted Amanda's shoes. 'Sniff the shoes, César.'

Caesar, not knowing what Juanita wanted of him, lowered his head and tried to lick Juanita on the face.

'Well?' demanded Vargas. 'What does the dog say?'

'I am not sure,' Juanita confessed. 'I think César is a little confused, after being cooped up in the laundry for so long. But, from his reaction, I do not think there is a problem with this woman's shoes.'

'There is only one way to be certain,' said Vargas. 'Diego, bring me her shoes.'

Diego stooped and roughly yanked them from Amanda's feet.

'Not so rough there,' Amanda protested.

Ignoring her complaint, Diego brought the shoes to Vargas. At the same time, Vargas lifted his shirt to reveal a knife on a scabbard attached to his belt. He slid the knife out and held it up.

'I did not know you carried a knife,' Tommy said with surprise.

'I even sleep with my knife under my pillow, *amigo*,' Vargas responded. 'A knife was my first toy as a boy.'

First taking one shoe from Diego, Vargas slit open the heel, lopping off the rubber, which fell to the floor. He did the same to Amanda's second shoe.

'The dog was right,' he said with satisfaction. 'No explosives there.' He motioned to Diego. 'Return the dog and the woman to the laundry. Tommy, you and I will take the reporter to meet *el padrino*.'

He tossed Amanda's shoes aside, then frogmarched her to the small lift. The three of them stood in silence as it began to ascend. Amanda's mind returned to the encounter in the garage. She had achieved her objective. Her scheme had worked even better than she'd hoped. Not only had she been brought to the Green Parrot's hide-out, she had found Caesar. Now, all she had to do was bluff her way out of this place again and alert Ben to where Caesar was being kept.

The lift doors opened, and Amanda was walked twenty metres before her blindfold was removed. She was left, blinking, looking at a man with an Elvis hairdo.

'We have a guest for you, *Padrino*,' said Vargas.

Carlos Marron turned in his seat and looked Amanda up and down. 'So, you are the Australian journalist.'

'And you are the Green Parrot,' Amanda replied.

'Maybe.' He gestured to a black leather sofa across from him. 'Sit. We talk.'

Tommy pushed Amanda forward, and she moved to the sofa and sat down facing the one they were calling *padrino*. 'There is a small tape recorder in my bag,' she said. 'I need it for the interview.'

The gang leader shook his head. 'No tape recorders.'

'Could I have a pen and paper, then, please? To take notes.'

Again, he shook his head. 'No, use your memory. If you are truly a good reporter, you will remember what I have to say.'

'Fine.' Amanda looked around the room. Vargas and Tommy stood leaning against the wall, their arms folded. 'I guess I have no choice.' Her eyes came to rest on the bank of screens. 'You watch a lot of TV?' she asked.

'It is my link with the world,' he replied. 'I have access to every television network there is.'

'Impressive,' said Amanda, deciding it would be best to flatter him.

'What questions do you have for El Loro Verde? In your article, you said that you wanted El Loro Verde's side of the story.' He sat back and folded his arms, looking at her intently. 'So, ask away.'

There had been no photographs of the Green Parrot available when Amanda had done her background research on the crime lord. But, from descriptions she had read, especially of his Elvis hairstyle, she was pretty certain this was her man.

'Tell me about your childhood,' she began. 'Is it true that you were born and raised here in Monterrey?'

The crime lord took a swig from a bottle of Perrier water. 'When I was a teenager, Monterrey was the richest city in Mexico. All the big multinational corporations that operated in this country had their head offices here. Many rich people lived in Monterrey, too – in fabulous mansions behind high walls along tree-lined streets. As a boy, I would walk those streets and dream about one day having a mansion of my own, just like those ones. I vowed that when I did I would bring my mother to live in my big house and she would never have to cook another meal in her life.'

Amanda tried to look sympathetic. 'That was an honourable ambition.'

'One day, I was walking along one of those streets, daydreaming as usual, when a woman ran out from her mansion. She told me to get rid of a battered old car that had been left in the street outside her house. She said it made her property look *feo*. This means "unsightly". That is a word you did not hear where I grew up, in the poor parts of Monterrey. There, everything is unsightly in the eyes of the rich, but we poor people did not know it.' He laughed to himself. 'She offered to pay me, so I left and came back with my cousin Rodrigo's tow truck. I took that wreck of a car away and dumped it out in the countryside.'

'Did the woman pay you, as she promised?' asked Amanda.

'Oh, *sí*, she paid me a lot of money. It must have been the equivalent of around three hundred American dollars. I gave fifty to Rodrigo for the use of his truck and kept the rest for myself. Back then, it was more money than I had seen in my whole life.'

'I can imagine.'

'This experience, it gave me an idea. The next night, I towed that same wrecked car back to the city, to a street in another wealthy part of Monterrey. The next day, I knocked on the door of the house where I had dumped the car. I told the maid I would tow the wreck away for six thousand pesos, which is about about five hundred American dollars. She came back from her mistress with the money. Can you believe it?! Rich women have no concept of haggling – I would have done it for one hundred dollars. So I towed the wreck away, and that night I dumped it outside someone else's door.'

Amanda nodded. 'Very cheeky of you.'

'And so it went, every day dumping the wreck outside a rich person's house, always at a new location. The rich people almost always paid me to remove the wreck from outside their houses. "Unsightly, unsightly, unsightly," they would say! This became such a good business for me, I employed my brothers and cousins to work for me, paying them a fraction of what I was making.

'But it did not last. Nothing in life lasts. Eventually, the rich women paid the police less than we were asking – to put a stop to our dumping business. But by that time I had made a lot of money. This was the start of my fortune and my cartel.'

'This was how Árbol was born?'

Marron nodded. 'That was the start of Árbol.'

'What happened if the rich people refused to pay?' asked Amanda, not knowing if she really wanted to hear the answer.

Marron shrugged. 'If they would refuse to pay, or agree to a deal but then not pay up once we had kept our part of the bargain and taken the wreck away, all the windows of their mansion might have rocks thrown through them, or the house would catch fire in the night. Once people heard of what we were capable of, it was only a fool who messed with us.'

'And from this beginning you moved into other criminal rackets?'

'It was from this experience with the car wrecks that I realised the potential of what I had stumbled upon. They say that some of the greatest scientific discoveries have been made by accident. By pure chance, I had discovered a way to make a lot of money from rich people. I had been in the right place at the right time. Opportunity came knocking, and I grabbed it. After that, we expanded our operations. We offered rich people our protection.'

'Protection from what?'

'From us!' Marron laughed. 'And from other gangs like us.'

'You were extorting money from them?' By now Amanda had no doubts that this guy was who he said he was, that he was genuinely Carlos Marron, the Green Parrot.

'Extorting?' Marron shook his head. 'We called it "neighbourhood support". If they refused our support, their homes or their businesses would unfortunately burn to the ground.' He faked a look of compassion. 'Very sad!' Then he produced a wide grin. 'We also took rich people on little holidays until we received money for their return.'

'You mean you kidnapped them for ransom?' said Amanda.

'We like to call it "liberation expenses". And when I had made a lot more money, I decided to build my mansion, right here. I was born in a shack at the end of this very street, you know. This would be the best house in the worst neighbourhood of Monterrey. But it is *my* neighbourhood. This is where I was born and raised. Everyone knows me. I am one of them. No one in this district rats on El Loro Verde. They know I will look after them if they look after me. And they know that if they betray me, I will make them and their families suffer.'

He said this with such nonchalance that it sent a chill down Amanda's spine. 'And your mother?' she asked, changing the subject. 'She moved in here with you, as you had always planned?'

Marron suddenly looked sad. 'Unfortunately, my dear mother passed away before this house could be completed. That is my dear departed mother.'

He pointed to a large painting on the wall. It was a portrait of a small woman with grey hair and a warm smile. She was so short that her feet did not touch the ground as she sat in a golden, throne-like chair. To complete the picture, the artist had given Mrs Marron a saint-like halo. A vase of fresh flowers stood on a side table below the portrait.

'We give her fresh flowers every day,' Marron added.

'It's as if your mother is always here with you,' Amanda said, faking sympathy. It appeared this crime lord's soft spot was the memory of his mother.

'Exactly. So, now you know how I came to create Árbol. The profit made from Árbol's business enterprises is distributed throughout the local community. I employ thousands of fellow Mexicans and keep them from starving. I am truly a friend of the people.'

'And you run your empire from this room?'

Marron paused, glancing at his watch. 'The internet has changed much, and my business has changed with it. Árbol now extends across Mexico, across the United States and Canada, across South America, across Europe. And you know the business of which I am most proud?' He looked around to Vargas. 'Take her to see the C-Room.'

Vargas walked over and grabbed Amanda by the arm.

'But I have more questions for you,' she protested.

'Maybe later,' Marron said. 'I have a teleconference coming up with associates.' He waved her away.

Vargas and Tommy took her to the floor below. The lift doors opened to reveal a room which almost occupied the entire second floor. It was packed full of computer equipment, with wires trailing everywhere. The curtains on the windows were drawn, and two pale young men barely out of their teens were sitting on large plastic balls in front of banks of at least twenty screens.

Amanda noted two Heckler & Koch MP5 sub-- machine guns lying on a bench. During her journalistic career, Amanda had written extensively about Special Ops soldiers such as Charlie Grover and Ben Fulton, and she knew that the MP5 was the favoured weapon of Special Forces units around the world for 'close quarters' operations. During her research on the Mexican crime cartels, Amanda had read that several of them, including Árbol, had either stolen or illegally purchased MP5s and similar military hardware from the Mexican Army.

'This is C-Room,' said Vargas. Keeping hold of her arm, he led Amanda to the screens.

Some screens displayed websites, some were full of ever-changing computer data, while others projected the footage from the many CCTV cameras dotted around the Green Parrot's compound. Seeing this, Amanda tried to memorise which areas of the mansion were being monitored by taking in the images on the screens. Then she recognised a homepage on one of the monitors. 'Friends of the People,' she said.

'That is us,' Vargas said proudly. 'This is an Árbol propaganda website, controlled from this room by these two guys, Cisco and Pancho. It is our secret.'

'Why reveal that to me? Tomorrow I could tell the world that you're behind Friends of the People.'

Vargas smiled. 'Tomorrow we could have another website or another dozen websites. People, young people especially, tire of old websites and are always looking for something new.'

'Is that what the Green Parrot is so proud of?'

'No, not that. Come see.' Vargas led her to a stack of computer servers that took up just a square metre of space. '*This* is C-Share. You can download any e-book, any piece of music, any movie in the world, from this site – for free.'

'I've heard of C-Share,' said Amanda. 'It's an illegal website sharing pirated material, isn't it?'

'*Sí.* One of our legitimate businesses bought it off some Swedish youngsters who ended up in jail for infringing copyright. Half the free download trans-actions that occur in the world every day take place on these servers.' He patted the stack. 'Amazing, huh?'

'Those servers handle all that online traffic?' Amanda was shocked at how little space they took up. 'But, if the downloads are free, how do you make money from it?'

Vargas shrugged. 'We don't. There is some paid advertising on the site, but C-Share still loses money. El Loro Verde doesn't care. He is happy that, through him, the poor people of the world have free access to all that stuff the big corporations pump out for rich people to buy. He is a modern-day Robin Hood, robbing the rich to share with the poor.'

'But if everyone uses pirated material rather than paying for it, people will stop creating new material. Without payment for copyright, there will be no new books or music or movies.'

Vargas shook his head. 'Copyright is just legal mumbo jumbo. Hollywood makes billions. They can afford a few free downloads. They will always churn this stuff out.'

'Not if no one pays to see it or hear it. And most of the people of the world *can* afford to pay a little,' argued Amanda. 'Free file sharing is theft. What if you spent months writing a book or recording a song, and someone else put it on the net so there were a million downloads but not a soul paid you for it? Would that be fair? Would that enable you to make a living? Of course not. There has to be reward for effort.'

Vargas shrugged. 'El Loro Verde is the boss. He can do whatever he likes.'

Amanda shook her head. She could see that she was not going to get anywhere with this man.

'Hey, Cisco,' said Vargas, 'put on your telephone voice for the *señorita*.'

One of the geeks, a pimply, bespectacled youth, grinned. He turned to Amanda. 'Miss Ritchie, this is hotel reception. Please do not be alarmed, but there is a fire emergency in the hotel, and the fire alarm is not working.'

Amanda's mouth dropped open in surprise. 'You're the one who called me.'

'So,' said Vargas, 'now we will return you to the hotel and you will write an article about all the good work that El Loro Verde is doing for the poor people of the world, and you will make sure that it is published widely.' He pulled the blindfold from his pocket.

Amanda was reluctant to leave before she got more information about where Caesar was being held. 'I still have questions for him,' she said, trying to stall her departure.

Vargas shook his head. 'You have asked enough questions. Now, keep your part of the bargain – write your article, make El Loro Verde look good.'

Tommy grasped Amanda's arms from behind, startling her. Vargas quickly fastened the blindfold over her eyes.

'Take her back to the Hilton,' he commanded Tommy.

Fifteen minutes later Amanda was shoved from the back of the van, her handbag thrown out after her. As the van roared away, Amanda staggered then caught her balance. Ripping the blindfold from her head, she saw that she had been deposited across the street from her hotel, on the Boulevard Antonio L Rodriguez. Turning, she tried to catch a glimpse of the fast disappearing van. It was a black VW, but its registration plate was smeared with mud and was unreadable. Within moments it had turned a corner and disappeared into the night.

With a sigh, Amanda picked up her bag and crossed the road to the hotel. The lone staff member at the front desk watched her with a look of surprise on his face; he rarely saw guests come in during the early hours of the morning without shoes on. When she reached her room, Amanda took out her phone and placed a call while sinking into the bed.

'Hey, what's up?' came a familiar voice.

'Sorry to wake you, Ben, but I've been abducted by the Árbol cartel,' she said, her voice quavering a little.

'What?' Ben almost yelled in alarm. 'Amanda, are you okay? Where are you?'

'I'm fine. They've just dumped me back at my hotel. But I saw Caesar, Ben!'

'You did?' He bombarded her with questions. 'Where? Was the Green Parrot there? Was Caesar all right when you saw him? They haven't hurt him?'

'Well, I didn't exactly see him. I was blindfolded at the time. But I know it was him. They had a woman who seemed to be in charge of him, and she called him César.'

'That sounds like the Mexican police dog handler who was kidnapped.'

'She got him to search me for explosives. And he recognised me, Ben. He knew it was me. The Green Parrot has definitely got him and is using him as a canine bodyguard.'

'Did you see the Green Parrot himself?'

'Yes, I had a long conversation with him. And I saw where he's hiding out. From the inside, anyway. It was about a ten-minute drive from the hotel.'

'I'm on my way to you now. Don't leave your room, and don't let anyone in but me.'

'Don't worry, I'm not going anywhere.' Amanda looked down to see that her hands were shaking. Shock was setting in. 'Please hurry, Ben. In case they come back for me.'

Ben was at Amanda's hotel within ten minutes, driven there through the city's deserted streets and past military checkpoints by a yawning Monterrey taxi driver.

When he knocked on the door to her room, she called nervously from the other side, 'Who is it?'

'It's okay, Amanda, it's me – Ben,' he replied.

'Are you alone?'

'Roger that.'

Even so, she checked through the spy-hole in the door. Only once she'd satisfied herself that he was alone did she open the door. As soon as she saw him standing there she burst into tears and threw her arms around him.

Still locked in her embrace, Ben worked his way into the room, kicking the door closed behind him with one foot. In the middle of the room, he pushed her back so that he could see her face.

'Don't cry,' he said, wiping her damp cheeks with the back of his hand. 'It's okay now.'

'I'm sorry,' Amanda snuffled. 'I've been to more war zones than I can remember, and have been in some pretty tight situations, and I thought I was pretty tough. But being hijacked by the Green Parrot's goons really put the wind up me.' Her hands began to shake again. Pulling Ben close again, she lay her head on his broad shoulder. 'There was no guarantee they were going to set me free.'

'I know.' Ben patted her on the back reassuringly.

Finally, Amanda took a deep breath, then stood back and smiled up at him. 'I'm fine now. I don't know what came over me.'

'The shock of what you went through is starting to set in,' he said. 'You should take it easy. Rest. Lie down.'

'At least we've tracked down Caesar. But the place is a fortress, and the Green Parrot has plenty of armed men guarding him there.'

'Well done, you.' Ben steered her to a chair. 'On my way over here I called Captain Lee. She's activating the unit. GRRR will be here in Monterrey and good to go in after Caesar within sixteen hours. And if we can capture the Green Parrot in the process and deliver him up to the Mexican Government, that will be a bonus.'

'That's fantastic!' said Amanda.

'In the meantime, we have to figure out his precise location. You said that the Green Parrot's hide-out was a ten-minute drive from here?'

Amanda nodded. 'It's a massive concrete place, like an office building, complete with a lift. And one floor is devoted to a massive computer set-up. They call it the C-Room. They're operating a pirated file-sharing business from there. The computer power in that room is phenomenal.'

'Interesting,' said Ben, deep in thought. 'You know,

computer servers give off high-frequency electronic waves that can be picked up by airborne equipment operated by U-2 spy aircraft for America's National Security Agency. They deny this type of hardware exists, of course, but they use high-flying spy planes to track down military and terrorist computer servers. The more servers, the more likely a spy satellite or U-2 will pick them up. If they're hidden in an underground bunker they'll be harder to locate. Was this C-Room underground?'

'No, on the second floor, I think.'

'Did the room have windows?' asked Ben.

Amanda pictured the C-Room in her mind's eye. 'It had windows, but the blinds were drawn. I don't think it ever sees the light of day.'

'Windows mean glass. The high-frequency electronic waves from the computer servers are transmitted through glass much more easily than through concrete or brick. The NSA electronic sensor should be able to pinpoint the Green Parrot's compound. The electronic waves would light up the building on the NSA screens just like an infrared picture. With so many servers there, the entire building would glow on the NSA monitors.'

Amanda was shocked. 'Wow. I never knew anything like that existed. And I'm a pretty good investigative journalist.'

'Classified information,' said Ben, taking out his phone and tapping in a number. 'I never told you about it.'

'Who are you calling?' asked Amanda.

'Captain Lee – to get the UN to ask for the NSA's help on this one. We need to pinpoint the location of the Green Parrot's building so that GRRR can go straight in as soon as the team is assembled here in Monterrey.'

CHAPTER 19

There was a chill in the night air as the members of GRRR pulled on black night-time combat gear provided by the US Navy SEALs – boots, trousers, shirts, bullet-proof vests, balaclavas and Kevlar helmets.

Two members of Australia's SAS Regiment, Sergeant Charlie Grover and Trooper Bendigo Baz, had been in Hawaii advising a new SEAL team on covert operations when they had received the GRRR operational activation call from Captain Lee. To get to Monterrey, they had hopped on the first USAF transport plane heading out of Honolulu for California, before catching another USAF lift across the border to Mexico. With them, they had brought aluminium travel crates containing Special Forces weapons and equipment on loan to the UN from the SEALs. Charlie was to lead the op on the ground, an op which Captain Lee had given the codename of Operation Green Parrot.

The three American members of the regular GRRR team had been the first to reach Monterrey – Sergeants

Duke Hazard and Tim McHenry, and signaller Brian Cisco. Sergeant Angus Bruce and Corporal Chris Banner had flown in next, all the way from England. Sergeant Jean-Claude Lyon came straight from the French Foreign Legion base on the Mediterranean island of Corsica. On the same French Air Force Hercules C-130 that brought him to Mexico, Lyon had been accompanied by Casper Mortenson and Willy Wolf. To complete the team, a Japanese Self Defence Force transport aircraft had brought Toushi Harada from Tokyo.

Ben Fulton, the twelfth member of the team, stood looking over Toushi's shoulder as the Japanese corporal rapidly tapped away at a computer. They were all gathered in a Mexican Air Force cargo hangar at Monterrey International Airport.

'There it is, Ben,' said Toushi, sitting back and pointing to the screen as a panoramic image appeared. 'You see?'

Ben leaned closer to the screen. 'How about that,' he said, half to himself. 'I'd heard all about the hardware that could sniff out computer servers, Toushi, but I'd never seen their work before.'

The image was taken from an American U-2 spy plane flying at 70,000 feet above Monterrey, well beyond the sight and hearing of anyone on the ground. It showed a group of buildings in northern Monterrey. The natural and man-made features were all depicted in blue, but one building glowed orange. With a one-time password passed on to him by Captain Lee, Toushi had gained access to the images coming from the U-2. At Liberty Lee's request, the NSA had diverted a U-2 training flight over northern Mexico and had turned on its sensors.

'The electronic sensor on the U-2 has found many office buildings in Monterrey with computer servers.' Toushi went on to explain that this was to be expected in a city with a population of several million. But this building was in a residential area and it had the highest output of delta rays from servers of any building in Monterrey; more servers and much more online activity than any other building here. 'I calculate it is roughly a ten-minute drive from the hotel of Amanda Ritchie. There is no doubt that this is the building that Amanda Ritchie was taken to. This is the building where she found Caesar.'

Charlie came over to join them. 'Is that the target building?' he asked.

'That's it, Charlie,' said Ben. 'Conveniently with a flat roof.'

Charlie nodded. 'There's a guard tower on the roof,' he pointed out. 'If we're going to take them by surprise, we'll have to HALO onto that roof and take out the tower, rather than land by heelo or rappelling down from one. Toushi, can we get an infrared look at the top of that tower?'

'Sure thing, Charlie.' Toushi tapped on his keyboard, bringing up an infrared image of the scene taken from the belly of the U-2 circling twenty-one kilometres above them. Now the features on Toushi's screen were in green. In the guard tower, two red humanoid shapes could be seen. The infrared camera in the U-2 was picking up the heat emitted by the pair of humans and was highlighting them against the green background.

'Two Árbol sentries,' said Charlie.

'There's no movement from either of them,' Ben observed. 'They could be asleep.'

'It'll be handy if they're still asleep when we drop in on them.' Charlie's attention was then caught by a large, bulky shape on the eastern side of the roof, away from the street. 'What's that?'

Ben bent down for a closer look. 'Something covered by a tarpaulin, maybe. Can't make out what it is.'

'Whatever it is, it shouldn't pose a problem for us,' said Charlie. 'Just be sure to avoid it when we go in.' He turned to the rest of the team. 'Okay, gather round, you blokes. Briefing time.'

The others formed a semicircle around Charlie, Ben and Toushi.

'Is that the target, Grover?' Duke Hazard asked, chewing gum furiously and nodding toward the image on Toushi's laptop.

'Roger to that,' said Charlie. 'I want all of you to take

a look at it and familiarise yourself with it once the briefing's over. Okay, so this is how the op is going to go down. Ben, Baz and myself will HALO in from a Mexican Air Force Herc and secure the roof, taking care of the guards in the watchtower.'

'Why are only three of you doing the HALO, if you don't mind me asking?' said Angus Bruce.

'There will only be room enough for three of us to land up there,' Charlie replied. 'We will be Alpha Team. Duke will lead Beta Team, with Tim, Brian and Willy. Beta Team will come over the front wall once we've signalled that the roof is secure. Angus, you will lead Gamma Team, with Chris, Casper and Jean-Claude. You guys will come over the back fence at the same time. Toushi, you will remain here to control comms, under the codename Birdcage.'

'How long have we got that coverage, Charlie?' asked Tim McHenry. He nodded toward Toushi's screen.

'We'll be losing the U-2 before long,' Charlie replied, 'but Captain Lee has arranged for SOCOM to send us an EC-130 EITS down from Arizona to monitor the target from just before zero hour, sending Toushi infrared images.'

The EC-130 was a version of the C-130 Hercules aircraft adapted to serve as an electronic 'eye in the sky'.

'Toushi will keep us abreast of what he can see from the EITS,' Charlie continued, 'and will maintain contact with the local police and the Mexican military via Lieutenant Peters, who will be going in with Beta Team to coordinate local police in the area.' He nodded to the police lieutenant, who was also pulling on black Special Forces gear. 'Lieutenant Peters is providing the ground transport for Beta and Gamma Teams.'

'But my Mexican colleagues won't be told about the operation or its targets,' said Peters. 'They must remain ignorant of such details.'

'Good idea,' said Sergeant Hazard, slapping a magazine into his SIG Sauer pistol. 'We don't want anyone tipping off the cartel.'

'Let's be clear,' said Charlie. 'Beta and Gamma Teams need to keep the bodyguards distracted while Alpha enters the house from the roof and goes from floor to floor looking for our two targets – Caesar and Carlos Marron. It's Alpha Team's job to secure them. Any questions?'

'Yeah, man, I got a question for you,' said Chris Banner, a lanky West Indian whose easygoing manner belied his role as a tough Special Forces operator. 'How many bad guys are we expecting?'

Charlie turned to Ben for an answer.

'Amanda Ritchie tells me she counted five Árbol people inside the house with the Green Parrot,' Ben advised. 'That's not counting the two guards we can see on the roof and any others likely to be inside the house or patrolling the grounds. We should be prepared to be opposed by at least ten or a dozen of these blokes all up.'

'Just how well trained they are with their weaponry, we don't know,' added Charlie. 'We go in taking nothing or no one for granted, and expect that they will be prepared to shoot to kill.'

'How are they armed?' asked Tim McHenry, as he fastened the equipment pouches onto his belt.

Again, Charlie turned to Ben for the answer.

'Amanda saw semi-automatic pistols and MP5s,' Ben advised.

'Snap!' said Bendigo Baz. He was toting an MP5 and had a Browning Hi Power semi-automatic pistol strapped to his right thigh. 'Sadly, I'll have to leave my good mate Mr Minimi behind on this little excursion.'

'Yes, no room for a Minimi inside the target building,' said Charlie. Everyone on the team knew the Belgian-made FN Minimi machinegun was Baz's preferred weapon. It was almost as long as the diminutive Australian was tall.

'Any chance that this place could be booby-trapped, Charlie?' Jean-Claude asked.

Charlie shook his head. 'No way of knowing, mate.'

'That's usually where Caesar comes in,' Ben remarked, bringing nods and sympathetic looks from his companions.

'Don't worry, Ben, we'll get your wee doggie back for you, old chum,' Angus assured him.

'We'll be taking plenty of flash-bangs and tear gas in with us,' said Charlie, 'so it will be full masks and headgear all round. Understood?'

'Copy that,' said Hazard, speaking for them all.

'Now, so there's no confusion, we will refer to target number one in all comms by his actual name – Caesar. Marron is target number two, and his codename for the op is Elvis.' This brought smiles all around. 'We want Elvis alive and kicking. There is no recent photo of him, but he is described as having an Elvis Presley brush-back hairstyle. It's likely that there will be another hostage with Caesar – Sergeant Juanita Del Ray, a dog handler from the Mexican Police. Keep an eye out for her. She is also to be extracted with Caesar if we come across her. Codename for her is Aztec.'

'Aztec,' Baz said with a nod. He repeated the codenames to himself to lodge them in his mind.

'Any questions?' Charlie cast his eyes around the team.

'What's zero hour, Grover?' Hazard asked.

'Zero hour for the air insertion is 0300 hours,' Charlie advised. 'Let's synchronise watches.' They all looked at their watches. 'On my word, it will be 0137 hours . . . Now!'

All their watches now showed the exact same time.

'Check comms,' Charlie then instructed, and each man tested his personal radio. Signaller Brian Cisco and Toushi tested the HF radios they would be using to keep in touch with the teams throughout the op.

'All good to go, Charlie,' Brian advised.

'Okay, let's get this show on the road and retrieve Caesar,' said Charlie.

'Roger that!' the others chorused.

As members of the team moved closer to take a look at the satellite image and familiarise themselves with their target, Charlie turned to Ben and Baz. 'Let's get kitted up for the jump.'

'Time to become Mexican jumping beans,' said Baz, commencing to inspect the Mexican Air Force parachutes that had been laid out on a bench. He, Charlie and Ben would each choose two parachutes for the jump.

Charlie, meanwhile, consulted with Toushi about the GPS coordinates for the Green Parrot's compound.

'U-2 go home now, Charlie,' Toushi advised, pointing to his blank screen.

'It's given us all we need to know,' Charlie said as he fed the compound's location into a trio of Navy SEAL portable GPS devices. About four times the size of a large wristwatch, these waterproof devices were designed to be strapped on the arm. Charlie handed one each to Ben and Baz, retaining the third for himself.

At the request of the UN, the Mexican Air Force was providing a C-130 for the parachute jump. With its four Allison turboprop engines roaring and propellers whirring, the Hercules rolled up to the Monterrey Airport hangar on schedule at 2.15 am and lowered its rear ramp.

'Our Tijuana taxi is here,' Baz joked.

'Good luck, you blokes,' Charlie called to the rest of the team. 'See you on the ground.'

Charlie led Ben and Baz out onto the tarmac and up the Herc's ramp. All three were clad in black from head to toe. They carried MP5s in a special pouch that hung from their belts, as well as holstered pistols, magazines and grenades in body pouches, and toted breathing apparatus. Stashed in pockets and pouches, all three carried several pairs of handcuffs provided by Lieutenant Peters. Each man now had a programmed GPS device strapped to his lower right arm. Over their shoulders they carried two parachutes each – a main chute and a reserve. Unlike the majority of their special ops parachute missions, the trio would not be spending days on the ground in hostile territory following the jump, so they weren't loaded down with bags of additional equipment and rations. This was to be a rapid in-and-out op.

As soon as they were aboard, the ramp was raised and the big transport plane crawled out along a taxiway.

Inside the cavernous interior of the Herc's cargo cabin, the three men were helped by a Mexican Air Force loadmaster to strap on their chutes. Then all of them, including the loadmaster, fitted breathing masks.

The C-130 could accommodate up to sixty-four airborne troops with their equipment, but it was also normal for smaller numbers of parachutists to be carried for special ops. As the trio settled into the webbed seating along the side of the fuselage, Ben's thoughts drifted to Caesar and how he would have loved to come along. Caesar enjoyed taking Hercules flights and absolutely adored making HALO jumps with Ben. If all went to plan, thought Ben, he and Caesar would be reunited within the hour.

From a standing start at the head of the main runway, the Hercules lumbered down the concrete and lifted gently into the night sky. Ben hoped that Caesar was being well treated by the Green Parrot and his men. If Sergeant Del Ray was with Caesar, Ben hoped that the handler was looking after his four-legged partner.

It took about ten minutes for the Hercules to climb to 30,000 feet and take station above northern Monterrey. As the aircraft circled the sky, its rear ramp lowered to the horizontal. Charlie, Ben and Baz formed up, facing the black void, their eyes on a red light on the fuselage wall beside the ramp. Before long, a half-moon came into view, glowing golden in the distance. Below, the lights of the sleeping city were visible. The loadmaster standing to the right of the ramp raised two fingers, indicating that it was two minutes before 3 am, zero hour – two minutes before jump time. The three jumpers tensed. With one finger, the loadmaster indicated there was one minute to go. Another sixty seconds ticked by. The red light turned to green. Zero! The loadmaster pointed to the night.

Without hesitation, all three jumpers ran along the ramp and launched themselves into space, clamping their arms by their sides once they left the Herc. As the aircraft flew on and away, raising its ramp as it went, the three soldiers went spearing toward the ground headfirst like superheroes in a Hollywood movie, accelerating up to 200 kilometres an hour in their freefall.

CHAPTER 20

A black dual-cab pick-up slowly pulled into the back street which ran behind the Green Parrot's compound and came to a halt. Inside the cab were four men and a boy of about ten. On the backs of their hands or on their necks, the men wore the plain star tattoo that identified them as members of the Estrella cartel. Among them was the cartel's chief, Antonio Lopez. Unlike Carlos Marron, who simply gave orders from his concrete compound and left his men to follow them through, Lopez liked to be actively involved in the more important operations of his organisation.

A former officer in the Mexican Marines, and later the Mexican Navy's elite FES Special Forces unit, Lopez had been trained to lead from the front. Just as he had personally checked out and planned the San Antonio hit on Rocky Marron, Lopez was coordinating his latest scheme from the front – an attempt to eliminate his chief competitor, Carlos Marron, the Green Parrot.

Lopez turned to the boy sitting beside him. 'You know what to do, José?'

'*Sí, Patrón*,' said the boy. This was the same José who had called out to Enrico Vargas, days before, in support of the Green Parrot. He had changed sides, becoming an Estrella supporter, telling the Estrella boss where to find the Green Parrot's residence.

From his shirt pocket, Lopez took a bunch of folded American twenty-dollar bills. He held them out to the boy. 'One hundred American dollars – your payment for the little favour you are about to do for me. Do not let me down.'

'I will not let you down, *Patrón*,' replied José.

'Now, after you place the backpack outside El Loro Verde's gate, walk away as casually as you can. As if you were going to church. *Sí?*'

'*Sí, Patrón.*' José took the money and stuffed it into a pocket in his shorts.

'Good boy. Soon, you will qualify to wear the star of Estrella, and be one of my trusted *pistoleros*.'

José beamed with delight. '*Sí, Patrón.*'

'Go. Get it done.' Lopez looked at the gangster sitting on the other side of José. 'Give him the backpack.'

The man stepped out of the car, and José scrambled after him. Reaching into the back of the pick-up, the gangster pulled out a bulky backpack and handed it to the boy. 'Take your time, little one,' he instructed. 'Do not run.'

As the man climbed back into the pick-up's cab, José

put the backpack over his shoulder then set off down the street.

Toushi sat alone in the hangar at Monterrey International Airport. Two Federal Police pick-ups had come and collected Beta and Gamma Teams, along with Lieutenant Pedro Peters, to transport them to the Green Parrot's compound for the early-morning assault.

'Birdcage, this is Mexican Air Force C-130,' reported the pilot of the Hercules that had transported Alpha Team. He spoke good English, the common language of international pilots. 'Your birds have flown and I am returning to base. I repeat, your birds have flown. Over.'

'Mexican Air Force C-130 from Birdcage, copy that,' Toushi responded. 'Thank you. Birdcage out.'

'Happy to help the UN, *amigo*. Mexican Air Force C-130 out.'

Toushi waited a moment, then said, 'Birdcage to all team. Please to report.'

'Beta Team in position,' Sergeant Hazard reported.

'Copy that,' Toushi replied.

'Gamma Team in position,' said Angus Bruce.

'Copy that,' Toushi acknowledged.

He checked his watch. Alpha Team – Charlie, Ben and Baz – would still be dropping like stones through the night sky toward Carlos Marron's house. They would open their chutes not far above the compound. Toushi smiled with relief – a predominantly green image had appeared on his previously blank computer screen.

'At last!' he said out loud. 'What take you so long?'

The image was similar to the last one transmitted by the U-2 spy plane, although this one showed more of the surrounding detail. It was an infrared view of Marron's compound and its neighbourhood. It was changing slightly in perspective with each passing second because it was being transmitted from the moving USAF EITS EC-130 as it circled high above the city.

Transmissions from the EC-130 had commenced fifteen minutes later than requested. It would turn out that the pilot had spotted the Mexican Air Force C-130 circling the target area in preparation for the jump by Charlie, Ben and Baz, and had kept out of the way until the Mexican plane left the area. With the jumpers in the air, the Mexican C-130 headed for base. Only then did the American EC-130 move into position and commence transmission of its infrared vision of the target area.

Toushi frowned and peered at the screen. 'What is this?'

The infrared image showed two human figures in the watchtower on the roof of the Green Parrot's compound, which Toushi was expecting. But now there was a third figure walking along the back street toward El Loro Verde's house. A small human figure – a child. Plus, Toushi could see that, south of the house, a vehicle sat parked in the street with heat glowing under its bonnet, indicating that the engine was running or had recently been running. Through the vehicle's windows, red blobs on Toushi's screen gave away the body heat of humans sitting inside it.

Toushi typed an instruction to the EITS camera, and the image on the screen zoomed out to a wider view. Now he could see the red figures of Lieutenant Peters and the members of Beta Team crouching around the corner from the Green Parrot's street, and those of Gamma Team in the street behind the compound, waiting for Charlie's command. Toushi spotted another vehicle with a hot bonnet at the northern end of the Green Parrot's street, also with people in the cab. Toushi flicked his 'transmit' button.

'All team, be advised – you got company on the ground.'

'*Patrón*, how can we be sure that the boy will identify El Loro Verde's house?' asked the driver, watching young José walk away.

The boy had been the first and only local to agree to identify the compound where El Loro Verde lived and, as far as the Estrella gangsters were concerned, there was no guarantee he was telling the truth or that he even knew where El Loro Verde lived.

'We will know when Marron comes rushing out,' said Lopez. 'He will have to either come this way and meet our guns, or go north and meet the guns of our men stationed at the far end of the street.'

'You are certain that Marron will panic, *Patrón*?'

'Oh, he will panic, Gomez. I know him too well. You will remember that I was in charge of his personal protection for years, until I broke from Árbol. We often practised getting him away from the scene of an attack to a new, safe location. That will not have changed. El Loro Verde will make a run for it, heading for a safe house somewhere else, and run right into our waiting guns. Before the sun rises tomorrow, El Loro Verde will be no more, and we shall commence moving in to take over Árbol territory. Bring up the telephone number, Gomez, but only call it when I tell you.'

'*Sí, Patrón.*'

In the dim light, Lopez and the others in the pick-up strained to watch José as he walked down the street. He stopped outside the largest house in the street, which was fronted by a high concrete wall and a large metal sliding gate. Keeping close to the wall beside the gate, and out of the view of a CCTV camera on the gatepost, José looked furtively up and down the thoroughfare.

Nothing moved in the street. All was quiet in the neighbourhood. Edging closer to the gate, the boy slipped the backpack from his shoulder and set it down in front of the gate. He took a step back.

In the pick-up at the end of the street, Lopez gave a command to his driver. 'Now, Gomez. Call the number.'

Gomez looked around at his boss with surprise. 'But the blast will . . .'

'Exactly. We want no witnesses, no one to tell the police who did this.'

Gomez shrugged. 'Okay, *Patrón*, whatever you say.' He pressed 'send'.

The silence was interrupted by the single ring of a mobile phone. José looked at the bag with surprise. In an instant, flame erupted from the backpack. Ball bearings, nuts and bolts scythed through the air, smacking into the gate and the wall. The phone had detonated an IED in the backpack. Moments later, the sound of the explosion reached the pick-up. A plume of smoke and dust rose from where the backpack had once been. José lay metres away, propelled across the street by the blast.

Lopez and his men clambered from their pick-up and prepared their weapons. Lopez smiled. 'Get ready to greet El Loro Verde, *amigos*.'

In the Green Parrot's house, all was mayhem. Vargas staggered from his room. Diego and Tommy were running past, each in his underwear and toting an MP5.

'What is happening?' Vargas demanded. Like the other two, he had been woken by the blast.

'Bomb at front gate,' Diego breathlessly replied.

'We got to get *el padrino* away!' called Tommy. He burst into Carlos Marron's bedroom.

Blinking in the sudden light, Marron and Lola sat up in their king-size bed. Rosa, lying at the foot of the bed, began yapping at Tommy.

'What is it?' said Marron, reaching for the Glock he kept on the nightstand.

'A bomb at the gate, *Padrino*,' Tommy informed him, scowling at the chihuahua. 'We got to go.'

'Is it the cops? The army? Or Estrella?' Marron said, half to himself. 'Tommy, tell Vargas to get everything ready. Lola, get your things. We're getting out of this place.'

'My jewels!' exclaimed Lola. 'I can't go without my jewels.' She dashed to the other side of the room and pulled a picture from the wall, revealing a safe.

'Tommy, bring the dog and the cop,' Marron added.

'There won't be room, *Padrino*,' Tommy protested.

'We will *make* room. We may need to exchange them for our freedom.'

Marron and his wife quickly dressed and grabbed a carry bag each. Lola crammed her bag with jewellery and shoved Rosa on top. Marron stuffed his to the brim with cash and some of his favourite Elvis records.

Once they were ready, Tommy escorted them to the roof at the run. They emerged into the night via a trapdoor that opened up and out. The flat rooftop was swathed in wisps of smoke from the bomb blast. Two very anxious Árbol *pistoleros* were on guard duty in the rooftop watchtower on the northwest corner. The tower consisted of waist-high concrete block walls topped by a tiled roof on posts. That tiled roof was almost entirely covered with satellite dishes. From the waist up, the sides of the watchtower were open to the elements. Both guards were equipped with M16 rifles, which they pointed at the street.

'What do you see?' Marron called to the pair. 'Is anyone trying to break in through the gate?'

'Nothing's happening, *Padrino*,' one guard replied. 'We can't see anything out there! Is it Estrella?'

'I don't know who it is. But what are they waiting for?' Marron turned to the southeast corner of the roof. There, Vargas had pulled a tarpaulin from the large unidentified object that the GRRR team had spied from the U-2. The large object was a black Bell Jet Ranger helicopter. Vargas jumped into the pilot's seat and began flicking switches. Before joining Árbol, he had flown Jet Rangers as a helicopter pilot with the Mexican Army. Back then, he had thought about perhaps getting a job in civil aviation once he left the military. He had never pictured himself as the lieutenant and personal pilot of one of Mexico's most wanted crime bosses. The helicopter's engine whined to life while overhead the rotors were beginning to turn.

With an MP5 in one hand, Diego escorted Juanita and Caesar up the stairs behind El Loro Verde and his wife. Juanita had Caesar on a short leash. When Caesar came out onto the roof, he stopped in his tracks. His nose was filled with the scent of explosive chemicals which filled the cool night air. It reminded Caesar of pitched battles with the Taliban in Afghanistan. The smell was so distracting that Juanita had to tug hard on his leash to get him to go with her toward the helicopter. 'Come, César!' she urged.

In addition to the pilot, a Jet Ranger could comfortably accommodate four passengers. Five humans and two dogs were about to fill the passenger compartment of this Jet Ranger.

'Hurry, hurry!' Marron urged Lola, clambering in first.

Lola was crying and clutching her bag. Rosa poked her head out, shaking with fear. Lola and Tommy followed Marron aboard the chopper. Once they were in, Diego pushed Juanita onto one of the plush leather seats, shoved Caesar in at her feet, then, clutching his submachine gun, clambered in on top of the sergeant, struggling to pull the door shut behind him.

'We are overloaded, *Padrino*,' called Vargas.

'No, we are not,' Marron yelled. 'You worry like an old woman. These things can carry much more than they are certified for. Get us up, Vargas! Get us away from here!'

'Where to, *Padrino*?'

'Cabo. To the Velásquez brothers. Let's go!'

Vargas nodded. 'Okay. Fingers crossed we can.'

With a *crack*, Ben's parachute snapped open and his chute pulled him up with a violent jerk. He was no longer a human missile. His shoulders absorbed the grip of the chute while his legs inclined toward the earth. The back streets of northern Monterrey spread below him. He checked the GPS on his arm. A glowing indicator showed that the target was to his left. As he turned his black silk chute in that direction, he spotted Charlie seventy metres away and about thirty metres below him. He knew that Baz would be around thirty metres above him – he had been the first to open his chute, and Ben and Charlie had deliberately dropped past him in the last stages of their freefall to ensure their landings were staggered.

Through the goggles of his SF-100 respirator, Ben saw the grey, concrete target building for the first time, to the south, as he descended gently toward it. Then, to his surprise, he saw a large black object lift off from one corner of its flat rooftop. He identified it as a Jet Ranger helicopter. He watched it rise into the air, nose down, tail high. It flitted away, still at an angle, flying south, before banking away to the west, gaining height as it went. Ben cursed to himself, guessing that the Green Parrot was probably making his escape. But was Caesar in the helicopter, too?

From the ground, along the street, a spurt of flame briefly lit the night. Someone down there was firing at the escaping heelo. But Ben couldn't worry about the helicopter – he had to concentrate on his landing. After that, despite the sight of the fleeing chopper, Ben, Charlie and Baz would still have to go through the task of securing the building and looking for their two targets. After all, there was no guarantee that either Marron or Caesar was aboard the heelo.

Reaching down, Ben unfastened the flap on the thigh holster containing his Browning Hi Power pistol, readying it for a quick draw. Ahead of him, Ben saw Charlie sweep in for a perfect landing on the eastern side of the rooftop. Ben was on course to land right behind him. He swooped in, then dragged on the control lines to bring himself to a halt. Just a metre above the roof, he hit the parachute release and dropped casually to the concrete. His chute fell away, sliding over the side of the building and out of the way.

As soon as he was down, Ben slid his Hi Power from its holster. The pistol would leave one hand free. Ben heard a familiar silken rustle from behind, telling him that Baz was landing. Ahead, Ben saw a watchtower on the northwest corner of the roof. Charlie was running around the northern side of the roof toward it with the slightly ungainly gait of his Zoomers. His MP5 was levelled and ready. Ben set off around the southern end of the roof, to approach the watchtower from the western side.

As Ben ran, he saw two figures in the watchtower. Both had been facing the street out front, expecting an assault to come from that direction in the wake of the bomb explosion. One *pistolero* was bringing an M16 rifle around to bear on Charlie. The SAS sergeant let off a three-round burst. The gunman dropped. The second Árbol sentry, slower to react than the first, was bringing his long-barrelled rifle around when he spotted Ben. As the sentry paused to take aim at him, Ben raised his Hi Power on the run. Before Ben or the sentry could fire, three rounds from an MP5 were let off behind Ben, and the sentry threw up his arms and fell, dropping his weapon. Looking around while on the run, Ben saw Baz on the eastern side of the roof, still in his parachute harness, with smoke curling from the end of the barrel of his MP5.

Antonio Lopez and his men were stationed behind their pick-up, using it as cover. Gomez, the driver, had an MP5 to his shoulder and was firing at the Jet Ranger as it passed overhead. Two other Estrella *pistoleros* were struggling to get their MP5s into operation.

'Get the devils!' Lopez cried, drawing a Glock pistol from his belt and letting off several rounds into the sky. 'Get them! Get them!'

Almost as soon as it had come swooping away from the compound, the helicopter had whizzed noisily overhead and disappeared to the west.

'We didn't think of that, did we, *Patrón*?' said Gomez, lowering his submachine gun. 'We didn't expect Marron to have a helicopter. What now?'

Before Lopez could answer, another voice rang out from behind them. 'Police! Lay down your weapons! Lay down your weapons, or we will shoot to kill!'

Swinging around, Lopez saw five figures in black running toward them from the southern end of the street. All wore black helmets and their faces were covered by goggles and face masks, which made them look like aliens. Four of the five had MP5s raised and pointing his way. The one doing the talking was armed with a pistol. This was the GRRR's Beta Team, accompanied by Lieutenant Pedro Peters of the Federal Police.

'Lay down your weapons and raise your hands!' called Lieutenant Peters. 'This is your last warning!'

'*Ándale! Ándale!*' yelled Sergeant Hazard.

'Don't fire!' Lopez yelled. Gingerly, he bent down and laid his pistol on the ground, then lifted his hands into the air. 'Do as they say,' he commanded his men.

Two of Lopez's men dropped their submachine guns and held up their hands. When Gomez hesitated, Duke Hazard let off a short burst with his MP5, sending dirt kicking up at the feet of the *pistolero*. Gomez got the message. He let the MP5 slip from his grasp and raised his hands. Seconds later, Lieutenant Peters and Beta Team were on top of the four cartel members, forcing them to the ground and locking their hands behind their backs with handcuffs clapped around their wrists.

'They are Estrella,' said Lieutenant Peters, spotting the trademark star tattoo on several of the gangsters. He rolled their leader onto his back to get a better look at his face. 'Lopez,' he declared with delight. 'It's Antonio Lopez, the leader of Estrella. We have made quite a catch, gentlemen.'

But Sergeant Duke Hazard didn't look happy. 'But not the catch we came here for.'

On the roof of the Green Parrot's compound, Charlie and Ben were kneeling, pressed against the eastern and southern sides of the watchtower wall. Baz, now free of his parachute, came running along the north side of the roof and vaulted over the tower wall. Inside the confined space of the tower, Baz scooped up the sentries' M16s and tossed them out. They fell to the ground several storeys below, landing with a clatter.

'This is Alpha Three,' came Baz's voice over their personal radios, his voice muffled a little by the face mask of his breathing apparatus. 'Two hostiles immobilised and disarmed. Will need medical attention.'

'Copy that, Alpha Three,' Charlie replied, similarly muffled. Charlie then changed to HF. 'Birdcage, from Alpha One. Receiving?'

'Birdcage receiving,' Toushi replied. 'Go ahead, Alpha One.'

'Rooftop secured. Two hostiles in need of medical attention. Over.'

'Copy that, Alpha One. There has been explosion at front gate, not related to operation. One child casualty. Heelo departed scene. Over.'

'Roger to that, we saw the heelo,' Charlie confirmed. 'Get the EITS to track it. Over.'

'Roger that. Birdcage on it. Over.'

'Alpha One, this is Beta One,' reported Sergeant Hazard. 'We got ourselves a situation here.'

'Go ahead, Beta One,' Charlie urged.

'Just arrested the boss of the Estrella cartel and three of his hoods, all taking pot shots at the heelo that overflew us. You want us to continue to execute the original assault plan?'

'Roger to that. Move up to the compound gate. There's a civilian there in need of medical attention. Get Willy onto that when the situation allows.'

'Roger that. Moving up to compound gate. Beta One out.'

'Alpha One, this is Gamma One,' reported Sergeant Bruce. 'In position and ready to move in on your word.'

'Copy that, Gamma One,' Charlie replied. 'Will advise. Birdcage, are you copying all this?'

'Roger that, Alpha One,' Toushi confirmed.

'Alpha proceeding to clear lower floors. Alpha One out.'

'Copy that. Birdcage out.'

Charlie returned to the personal frequency. 'Alpha Three, cover Alpha Two and me. We're going to the trapdoor.'

'Roger that.' Baz took up a position behind the watchtower wall with his MP5 aimed at the closed trapdoor. If anyone attempted to emerge from that trapdoor, Baz would blast them. 'You're good to go, Alpha One and Two.'

Charlie and Ben rose up and scurried to the trapdoor.

As both knelt beside it, Charlie signalled instructions to Ben by hand. Ben nodded, then removed a long, cylindrical CS tear-gas grenade from a pouch on his belt. At the same time, Charlie took out a flash-bang, an M-84 stun grenade, which looked much the same as the tear-gas grenade. Both removed the circular pins, and Charlie yanked the trapdoor open, then dropped the stun grenade in through the opening. Ben followed suit, delivering his tear-gas grenade. As the grenades bounced down the concrete stairs to the floor below, Charlie let the trapdoor drop shut again, and both men pulled back and bent low, clasping their gloved hands over their ears.

From below came the dull sounds of the grenades detonating. The flash-bang, which contained mercury and magnesium powder, burst with the bright, blinding flash equivalent to 300,000 candlepower, and a deafening concussion of 160 decibels – the engine of a jet fighter taking off emits 140 decibels. The combined effect of a flash-bang was to temporarily blind and deafen anyone in close contact with it. Ben's grenade, meanwhile, began emitting tear gas, which would quickly fill the stairway's landing and adjoining rooms, incapacitating anyone it reached who wasn't equipped with a respirator.

With ringing ears, Charlie and Ben waited crucial seconds, giving the tear gas time to spread. In the pause, Ben holstered his pistol and brought out his MP5, clapping a magazine into place and flicking on the torch fitted to the top of the sleek black submachine gun. Charlie likewise turned on the light atop his weapon, then reached over and opened the trapdoor. Ben immediately rose and entered the stairwell with Charlie following right behind him. Baz promptly jumped over the watchtower wall and ran to follow them down through the opening.

The tear gas had filled the stairwell by the time the trio descended. Wearing their respirators, they were unaffected by the gas. With Charlie and Ben covering him, Baz slipped past them and in through the first open doorway he came to. The other two followed him. They were in Marron's palatial living room, in complete darkness. Their torches lit up the leather couches, LCD screens and the portrait of Marron's mother. The trio checked the room and the adjoining kitchen, finding no one, before moving to each of the four bedrooms and bathrooms spread around the four sides of the building's living area. All the rooms were empty, with the bedrooms displaying signs of having only recently been vacated. Alpha Team moved back to the stairs.

'Alpha One, from Beta One,' came Sergeant Hazard's voice. 'In position at front gate.' He had left Lieutenant Peters with the four Estrella prisoners. 'Beta Four is attending the civilian casualty from the IED blast, who is still alive. Beta Team awaiting your "go". Over.'

'Copy that, Beta One. Alpha Team has secured the

top floor. Moving to next floor. Beta and Gamma Teams keep your eyes peeled for hostiles we flush out, trying to make a run for it. Alpha One out.'

'That's a roger from Beta One,' said Hazard. 'Out.'

'Gamma One to Alpha One, roger that,' said Angus. 'Gamma One out.'

Charlie turned to Ben. 'Do we know what's on the next floor down?'

'According to Amanda, it would be the C-Room,' replied Ben.

'That's right.' Charlie nodded, then pointed down the stairs. 'Baz, take the lead.'

'Roger the lodger,' Baz cheerfully responded. MP5 at the ready, and with the light of his torch piercing the darkness, Baz led the way down the next set of concrete steps.

When they reached the bottom, the C-Room spread to their right with its masses of computer equipment. All its screens were eerily aglow. There were two empty camp beds in a corner. A pair of MP5s lay on a bench, and Baz quickly took charge of them. Searching the room, the trio didn't find a living soul.

'I would have expected someone to have been in here monitoring the CCTV,' said Ben.

Charlie nodded. He looked around the room until his gaze fell upon the lift. Like all lifts, its closed metal doors had a series of numbers displayed above them, corresponding to the floors it served. The numeral '2' was glowing yellow. 'This would be the second floor, right?'

Ben nodded.

Charlie walked to the lift and pressed the down arrow, then levelled his weapon at the doors. They slid open, revealing Pancho and Cisco, cringing back against the lift wall with their hands in the air, quivering with fear.

'Don't shoot! Don't shoot!' the pair cried. They had been hiding in the lift ever since the bomb had gone off at the front gate.

They were hauled out of the lift and made to lie on the floor, where their hands were handcuffed behind their backs.

'How many more of you blokes are there in the building?' Charlie demanded.

'Maybe five or six,' Cisco replied.

'And where is the dog?' said Ben. 'Where is Caesar the labrador?'

'The dog?' Pancho looked confused. 'Vargas was keeping him in the laundry. Next floor down.'

'But we haven't seen him in a while,' added Cisco.

'Stay there, you two,' Charlie ordered the handcuffed pair. 'Make a move and it could be your last.'

'We won't go anywhere, *señor*,' Cisco assured him. 'We are not *pistoleros*. We don't even like guns.'

'Just geeks who play with computers,' Pancho added,

looking around at the three masked Special Forces soldiers with an imploring look on his face. 'Do not hurt us.'

'Stay put and you'll be hunky-dory,' said Baz.

'Please?' said Cisco, looking mystified. 'Who is this Hunky Dory?'

'Don't worry about it, mate,' said Baz.

Cisco smiled weakly. 'Okay, "mate".'

'Let's go,' said Charlie.

Leaving the two computer geeks in the C-Room, Alpha Team made their way down to the next floor. In the laundry they found a mat on the tiled floor. There, in the light of his torch, Ben located brown dog hairs on the mat.

'Caesar was here,' he declared, his chest tightening.

Their radios crackled. 'Alpha One from Gamma One,' came Angus's voice. 'Receiving? Over.'

'Alpha One receiving, Gamma One,' Charlie answered. 'Go ahead. Over.'

'We've just secured five hostiles trying to get away over the back fence. The wee brave Árbol guards were scared witless by your roof assault. Over.'

'Copy that, Gamma One. Alpha Team has secured three floors. One floor to go. Out.'

Now they knew where the remainder of the Green Parrot's bodyguards had disappeared to. Charlie led Ben and Baz in checking out the basement garage. All they found were Marron's abandoned Hummer, Ferrari and Porsche.

'Alpha One to Birdcage and all Betas and Gammas. Compound secured. Two prisoners, two hostile casualties. No sign of Caesar or Elvis.'

'Elvis has left the building,' Baz quipped beside him.

'Birdcage,' Charlie continued, 'what has the EITS told you about that heelo that got away? Over.'

'Alpha One from Birdcage. Heelo heading west. EITS continuing to track. Over.'

'Heading west? Okay. So are we. Out.'

CHAPTER 21

Caesar sniffed the room's earth floor. Behind him, little Rosa did the same. Rosa was mightily impressed by her new labrador friend. He showed little interest in her, but his superior manner gave Rosa confidence. Both dogs had been bundled into the mud-walled storeroom as soon as Carlos Marron and his companions had arrived at the small hilltop farm not far from the village of San Sebastian. Juanita was locked away in another adobe farm building. Marron and his party had been sent to this farm hide-out by fellow criminals the Velásquez brothers, who had their headquarters at Cabo San Lucas, a scenic seaside town popular with American tourists. Few tourists, or locals for that matter, ventured up into the dry, inhospitable hinterland.

Apart from the escape from the shed in the Green Parrot's Monterrey compound, Caesar had dug himself out of a room like this once before – in Afghanistan. He remembered how the soil had smelled differently at one particular part of the floor there, beside the wall, where it had been disturbed by human digging. Now, with his nose down, he went sniffing around the base of the wall. But he couldn't find a spot where the earth smelled softer. Still, it was sandy and easy to move, so Caesar decided to dig anyway. The earth was soon flying out behind him.

Rosa came to stand beside him and, emulating him, started scratching at the ground, although her tiny paws made little impression. Soon the bottom of the adobe wall gave way, with chunks of hardened mud partly filling the sizeable hole the labrador had made. Caesar set to work again and soon had removed the pieces of adobe. By the time he had finished, the hole was much larger than before. Pushing his head down and into it, he was able to see rays of moonlight outside.

Inspired by his success, Caesar kept digging, and after many minutes the hole was big enough for him to slither into. Midway through, with his head out and his tail still inside the storeroom, and with the soft soil filling in the hole around him, he became stuck. Snorting with frustration, he tried to pull himself free. Behind him, little Rosa tried to nudge him in the rump to help him forward, to no effect. Finally, with a monumental effort, Caesar was able to scramble from the escape tunnel and out into the open, his leash trailing behind him. Once he'd emerged, Rosa was able to walk through the hole with ease. But then she struggled to clamber up the other side; the walls of the hole were too steep for her.

Caesar studied his surroundings wearily. He could see a ditch running away into a field of blue agave plants, and this seemed to Caesar to offer the best escape route. He set off at the trot toward the ditch. Behind him, Rosa began to bark, calling for him to wait for her.

Nearby, Diego and Tommy jerked awake in their wicker chairs. Both were supposed to be on guard duty. Stationed by the farm's well, they could see the road to the farm and the black Jet Ranger, which sat on the flat a hundred metres away.

'What is that noise?' said Diego, raising his MP5.

'It's that stupid little Rosa,' said Tommy.

'Why is it barking?'

'It must have got out,' said Tommy. 'I suppose I will have to go and get it.' With a grunt, he came to his feet.

Caesar, seeing Tommy coming, dropped down onto his haunches and, with his head low, watched him. In the early morning light, and with his much superior night vision, Caesar could see Tommy but Tommy could not see Caesar. The *pistolero* walked right by him.

Tommy came to where Rosa was trapped at the end of the escape tunnel. Looking up at him with a fierce gaze, she yapped nonstop.

'Be quiet, rat dog!' Tommy growled. 'You would wake the devil. And how did you dig such a large hole?'

Reaching down, he picked her up. She immediately bit him on the wrist. With a howl, Tommy let go of the pink chihuahua. Rosa dropped free from his hands and landed on the ground. Caesar took advantage of the fact that Tommy, who was gripping his wrist and yowling with pain, was distracted. Rising up, the labrador quickly followed the ditch to the south, with Rosa trailing along in his wake. It didn't take long for the night to swallow the two dogs.

🐾🐾

Just after dawn, a Russian-built Mexican Air Force Mil M-8 helicopter set down outside a hangar at the Monterrey International Airport. Inside the hangar, the GRRR team members were shouldering their arms and equipment. They had all swapped night-time black for their regular daytime camouflage outfits, and Baz had happily reacquainted himself with a Minimi machinegun for the next phase of the operation.

Toushi took one last look at his computer screen. 'Still there, Charlie,' he called across the hangar. 'Still in San Sebastian.'

The EITS had tracked the Jet Ranger as it flew across northwest Mexico, then across the Gulf of California, to the town of San Lucas on the southern tip of the Baja California Peninsula at Cabo San Lucas. Shortly after, the Jet Ranger had flown on, heading several kilometres inland to San Sebastian.

Charlie gave a thumbs up in acknowledgement of Toushi's latest report, then turned to a group of his comrades. 'You say the boy will be okay, Willy?' He was referring to José, the boy caught in the blast.

'*Ja, ja*, he will be fine, Charlie,' said the medic as he stuffed bandages in his tunic pockets. 'Because of the way the IED was placed, most of the shrapnel went straight up in the air. The blast blew the boy across the street. He is battered and bruised, but he will live.'

'He must have put the bomb there in the first place,' said Tim McHenry. 'A kid should know better than to get involved with criminals.'

'Well, Antonio Lopez and the perpetrators of that IED are behind bars now,' said Lieutenant Peters. He was also sticking around for the next leg of the op.

'And, with luck, we'll have Caesar back before the day's out,' said Baz.

'I do hope so, mate,' said Ben. He'd succeeded in keeping a lid on his disappointment after just missing Caesar at El Loro's compound, but his heart was still aching for his four-legged friend.

'Okay, you blokes,' Charlie called to all the team members. He twirled a finger in the air. 'Time to get airborne.'

Determined to find Ben, Caesar was padding purpose-fully over the sandy soil. Behind him, with her short legs working hard, little Rosa was running to keep up. Several times she barked at him, urging him to stop and allow her to catch up. But the single-minded Caesar paid no attention – he had to locate his master.

Suddenly, Caesar stopped in his tracks. With his head cocked to one side, he listened intently. He'd picked up a sound familiar to him from both ops and training. He looked to the sky. Rosa now yapped at him, as if asking him what the delay was. But Caesar was focused on the distant sound. A minute or so later, three sleek helicopters passed overhead in formation. Flying at no more than 500 feet, they were US Army Apache AH-64 attack helicopters.

Following their course, Caesar barked at the choppers, as if calling to them: *Hey, guys, I'm down here! It's me, Caesar! Down here!*

The Apaches, lethal flying machines with missiles suspended either side of their tandem-seat cockpits, flew on. Caesar hoped they were looking for him. But they weren't. They were taking part in an exercise with the Mexican Army, and even if the heelos' two-man crews had seen the two dogs down below, they would have had no idea that one of them was a canine military colleague in need of help.

As he watched the three helicopters disappear, and as the sound of their engines faded away, Caesar stopped barking. He snorted, then looked at Rosa, who looked back at him. As he turned and once again set off in search of Ben, Rosa hurried after him.

🐾🐾

Mid-morning, the twenty-four-seat Mil helicopter landed the GRRR team three clicks south of San Sebastian. This time they were divided into two teams of six – Alpha and Beta, led by Charlie and Hazard. The heelo set the two teams down 500 metres apart on dry, sandy ground dotted with tall, prickly cactus plants.

Leaving the chopper to wait for them on the ground, and keeping the same 500-metre distance between them, the two teams began a fast-paced northerly yomp toward San Sebastian over rising, uneven ground. They regularly paused to check their GPSs and to rehydrate from their canteens in the blistering sun. By the middle of the day, the temperature hovered around forty degrees Celsius. Meanwhile, the glare bouncing up from the sandy ground made sunglasses mandatory.

They had been on the move for twenty minutes when a tinkling bell attracted their attention. Charlie waved his men down. Alpha Team went to ground, and on a rise in the distance Beta Team did the same. A rough track crossed Alpha's path, and before long a donkey with a tinkling bell around its neck appeared. A boy of eight or nine was riding it bareback, and a younger girl mounted behind him clung to his waist. Seeing the soldiers, the wide-eyed boy pulled the donkey up.

'Lieutenant, do you want to see what the children can tell you?' Charlie asked Peters.

The lieutenant moved to the donkey. He and the boy spoke for a few moments before the lieutenant motioned for Alpha to join them. On Charlie's command, Alpha Team rose up and surrounded the donkey and its young riders.

'The boy says they are going to school at San Sebastian,' said the lieutenant.

'They're a bit late for school, aren't they?' Baz remarked.

'No, in the more remote parts of Mexico, one lot of students goes to school in the morning and another group in the afternoon,' the lieutenant explained. 'This makes the most of teaching resources, and frees the children to help their parents on their farms or in their shops or market stalls during the other half of the day.'

'Tell the boy we're looking for a black helicopter,' said Charlie.

The lieutenant and the boy conversed again. 'He heard a helicopter last night – for the first time in his life,' Lieutenant Peters then said. 'He has seen them on the TV and in the movies, but this was the first one he has encountered personally. It flew over his farm and woke him. He thinks it landed nearby, at a neighbour's farm northwest of here.'

'Tell him we need him to lead us there,' said Charlie. 'Baz, you take charge of the kids.' He flicked his radio on. 'Beta One, from Alpha One. We have a suspect heelo sighting. Turning northwest to investigate. Follow my lead. Over.'

'Beta One copies. Roger that. Out.'

'Alpha One out.'

As Alpha turned northwest, so too did Beta.

The boy, whose name was Miguel, was delighted to become the soldiers' guide. Miguel turned his donkey around and, as Baz walked beside the animal, he took great interest in Baz's Minimi machinegun. Behind Miguel, his little sister Maria held out something to the Australian soldier. Baz always had an empathy with children, which probably had a lot to do with the fact that he was a big kid himself.

'It's a local confectionery,' said Lieutenant Peters, seeing Baz hesitate.

Baz took the sweet and put it in his mouth. 'Yum! What is that?'

'It is made from the cactus plant,' the lieutenant replied.

'Who would have guessed?' said Baz. '*Gracias*, little miss.'

Maria beamed back at him.

At the front of the column, big Chris Banner had taken point and was leading the way. Fifteen metres back in the line of troops, with the donkey in the middle of the column, Ben was walking with Charlie.

'We have to assume that El Lorro took Caesar with him in the Jet Ranger, Charlie,' he said, clearly worried about where Caesar might be.

'He seems to have also taken Sergeant Del Ray with him, mate,' said Charlie. 'So, where we find one, we're sure to find the other.'

'I hope you're right.'

After they'd gone a kilometre or so, Chris, topping a rise ahead, suddenly came to a halt and raised a hand. Charlie signalled the column to stop.

'Charlie, Ben,' came Chris's voice over their radios, 'you better come take a look at this.'

Charlie and Ben ran toward Chris at the double. On reaching the top of the gentle incline, they too came to a halt. Following Chris's pointing finger, both gawked in amazement. Forty metres away, a pair of dogs sat side by side on the track, looking back at them. One was a brown labrador, the other, a pink chihuahua.

'Caesar!' Ben exclaimed. 'Caesar, here to me, boy! Here to Ben!' He added a whistle, the 'Return quickly' signal.

Letting out a bark of recognition, Caesar jumped up and came running along the track. Rosa followed behind, yapping with each stride. When Caesar was three metres from Ben, he took a flying leap at him. Ben caught him in his arms, staggering as the labrador almost knocked him off his feet.

'It's all right, mate!' Ben laughed as Caesar began to frantically lick him. 'It's all right. We've found each other again! It's all right.'

CHAPTER 22

Consumed with anger, Lola paced back and forth outside the adobe farmhouse. 'How could you two let my Rosa run away?' she demanded.

'And the sniffing dog!' Marron railed, running a hand through his thick hair.

'They dug their way out, *Padrino*,' Tommy tried to explain.

'And it was dark,' said Diego.

'They dug their way out once before, you idiots!' growled Vargas. 'You should have taken precautions.'

'*You* were in charge of the prisoners, Vargas,' Marron exploded, turning on his deputy. 'It is just as much your fault.'

'Everyone, stay right where you are!' bellowed Lieutenant Peters. 'Drop your weapons and raise your hands.'

All eyes turned in the direction of the voice. Half a dozen heavily armed soldiers could be seen rising up from behind a low stone wall with their guns aimed at them.

'Do as he says!' Sergeant Hazard yelled from behind them.

Swinging around, the cartel members saw another half-dozen soldiers lining the crown of the farmhouse's roof at their backs, all with weapons trained on them. Beta Team had come around from the north and silently climbed up onto the roof.

Marron and Lola raised their hands. Tommy and Diego dropped their MP5s. But Vargas set off for the Jet Ranger.

'Get him, Caesar,' Ben commanded, letting him off the leash.

Caesar bounded after Vargas. Launching himself at Vargas's back, he brought his former jailer to the ground. Moments later, Ben and Lieutenant Peters were on the scene and Vargas was in handcuffs.

'Well done, Caesar!' said the lieutenant.

Caesar sat staring at Vargas, his tongue hanging out and a look of satisfaction on his face.

'Yes, well done, mate,' said Ben, pulling the brown labrador into a cuddle and giving him a vigorous pat.

Ben and Caesar were once more a team, and all seemed right with the world. Árbol and Estrella had lost their leaders, and Sergeant Juanita Del Ray had been located and freed. And soon the Green Parrot would have his very own cell at Monterrey's Apodaca Prison.

CHAPTER 23

'But what happened to the little pink dog?' Maddie asked from the back seat.

Nan and Maddie had picked up Ben from Sydney Airport on his return to Australia. Ben had arrived back with Amanda, who was getting a ride with them in Nan's little orange Ford Fiesta. Josh was in Holsworthy, preparing to play with his new band, which was called Sign of Seven.

'Rosa the pink chihuahua is now living on a farm in Baja California, with the family of Miguel and Maria, the children who helped us track down the Green Parrot,' said Ben.

'Good. But I wish Caesar had come back with you, Daddy,' Maddie responded. 'Does he have to stay in Mexico for quaramteem?'

'Afraid so, Maddie,' her father replied. 'It was tough parting with him again, but the Mexican Government is looking after him while I came home to see you all, and will only release him to me and no one else. There won't be a repeat of what happened in Texas.'

'That sort of mistake doesn't happen twice,' Amanda added reassuringly.

'And the big surprise, Ben, is that Josh has invited us to his band concert tonight,' said Nan.

'It's not a band concert, Nan,' Maddie corrected her. 'It's a gig.'

Nan smiled. 'Sorry, dear. His gig.'

'I'm looking forward to it,' said Ben. He turned to Amanda. 'I don't suppose you'd like to come? You could stay the night at our place. Is the spare bed ready, Mum?'

'Yes, dear,' Nan replied, 'but Amanda probably wants to get home.'

'No, no, I'm in no hurry to go home,' Amanda quickly responded. 'After my experience in Mexico, I haven't enjoyed being on my own at night. And I'd love to see Josh's band play.'

In the seat beside her, Maddie folded her arms and went quiet.

'Then it's settled,' Ben said with a smile.

🐾🐾

A crowd lined up at the door to the Holsworthy Community Hall. Several student bands were playing tonight, and the family and friends of band members were out in force.

Ben hadn't had time to change, so he was still in his

military fatigues as he and his party walked up to the door. Immediately, he was recognised by the new school principal, Mrs Piscari.

'Sergeant Fulton!' The principal beamed. 'How wonderful that you are in the country to see Josh play. I know what a busy man you are.'

'Really looking forward to it, Mrs Piscari,' said Ben. 'From what my mother tells me, Josh has developed a real talent for the drums.'

'And you've brought your entire family along, too.' Mrs Piscari held out her hand to Amanda. 'A pleasure to meet you, Mrs Fulton.'

Amanda flushed, embarrassed. 'Er, I'm not –'

'She's not my mummy,' Maddie declared. 'I've already got a mummy.' Letting go of Nan's hand, she pushed on ahead.

Amanda looked at Ben, who looked at Nan.

'We've been having some mummy issues while you've been away, Ben,' said Nan. 'You better go and sort that out before the performance.'

Ben hurried after Maddie and, catching up with her, took her hand. Soon, after a few words, Maddie was cuddling in close to her father.

'I'm so sorry,' said a flustered Mrs Piscari to Amanda. 'You and Maddie look so like mother and daughter.'

'That's okay,' Amanda responded, a little embarrassed. 'It's an easy mistake to make.'

'Maddie isn't ready for another woman in Ben's life just yet, Amanda,' said Nan as they continued on together. 'For that matter, neither is Ben.'

'We're just good friends,' Amanda assured her.

'Oh, I've seen the way you look at Ben, dear,' said Nan. 'You are very fond of him. He just hasn't woken up to that, yet. He's still in love with Marie, you see.'

'Ah . . .'

'Why don't you pull back a little? For the kids' sake. You can still be good friends, without complicating matters. Don't you agree?'

'Of course.' Amanda, doubly embarrassed now, didn't say any more. She took her seat and waited for the concert to begin.

'They were terrific,' said Ben, clapping as he came to his feet after the curtain fell.

'Can we go backstage to see them?' Maddie pleaded. 'Joshie told me we could.'

'Actually, I have to run,' said Amanda, giving Ben a quick peck on the cheek. 'Thanks for inviting me. I'll grab a cab outside and catch the train back to Sydney.' She glanced at Nan, and the pair of them shared a nod.

As Amanda hurried through the crowd toward the

door, Ben looked a little dazed. 'That's strange. I thought she was staying over.'

'Amanda is a busy woman, dear,' said Nan. 'Come on, let's go see the orchestra members.'

'They're a band, Nan,' Maddie corrected her. 'Remember? Not an orchestra.'

Nan looked at Ben and winked.

Backstage, they found Josh and his fellow band members packing away their equipment. When Josh saw his father approach, he suddenly looked worried. 'What did you think, Dad? Sick, huh?'

'Yes, son,' said Ben, patting him on the back. 'Brilliant. Loved it. You and your mates are so talented. Just do me a favour?'

'What's that?'

'Just because you're in a band, don't go getting any tattoos.'

'Tattoos?' Josh laughed. 'Nah, they're so old-fashioned. Old guys like Bendigo Baz have tattoos.'

Ben roared with laughter. His phone began to ring. Taking it out, he saw that the caller was Liberty Lee. 'Yes, Captain?' he answered.

'Hello, Sergeant Fulton. Rice for water.'

'Already? I've only just arrived home.'

'Can't be helped, I'm afraid. This operation is in the Caribbean. Briefing will take place on the island of St Thomas. Go via Mexico City and collect Caesar on the way through – the Mexican Government have agreed to release him from quarantine. Your travel details are being emailed to you. Good luck.'

'An op, dear?' Nan asked, as Ben slipped the phone back into his pocket.

'Yes, Mum,' he said. 'Sorry, kids.'

'What are you waiting for, Daddy?' Maddie pushed him toward the door. 'You and Caesar have work to do.'

LIST OF MILITARY TERMS

Apache AH-64	American attack helicopter with twin engines and a crew of two
Bell 412	transport helicopter that can carry up to thirteen passengers and has a crew of one or two
Bell Jet Ranger	civilian helicopter sometimes used by police and military
C-4	plastic explosive frequently used by military
clicks	kilometres
comms	communications
copy that	'I have received' or 'I understand'
CS gas	tear gas
EC-130	electronic surveillance version of C-130 Hercules aircraft
EDD	explosive detection dog
EITS (Eye in the Sky)	specialised surveillance aircraft equipped with standard and infrared video cameras and sensors, capable of remaining over targets for extended periods
flash-bang	stun grenade; incorporating bright light and sound effects
French Foreign Legion	French Army unit used for special operations; traditionally accepts foreigners without asking questions

Glock 17	Austrian 9mm semi-automatic pistol, widely used by law enforcement agencies and military around the world
HALO	high altitude low opening; parachute jump from high altitude followed by freefall, with the parachute opening at low altitude
HE	high explosive
heelo	helicopter, also written as 'helo'
Hercules, C-130	four-engine, propeller-driven military transport aircraft; pronounced 'Her-kew-leez' and often referred to as a 'Herc'
HF radio	high-frequency radio
hostiles	enemy fighters
Hunter Corps	special forces unit of the Royal Danish Army
ID	identification
IED	improvised explosive device or homemade bomb
insertion	secret landing of troops behind enemy lines
intel	intelligence information
LALO	low altitude, low opening; parachute jump from a low altitude

loadmaster	crew member in charge of cargo and passengers in military cargo aircraft and helicopters
M-8 Helicopter	Mil, Russian-made military helicopter – one of the most widely used helicopters in the world
M-16	American-made 5.56mm assault rifle
M-84	standard stun grenade used by US military
M&P40	Smith & Wesson .40 inch American semi-automatic pistol
MD 500 Defender	McDonnell Douglas helicopter, can carry up to five personnel
Mounties	Royal Canadian Mounted Police
MP5	Heckler & Koch 9mm German compact submachine gun, widely used by Special Forces and anti-terrorist units around the world
operator	Australian SAS Regiment soldier
op(s)	military operation(s)
Presidential Unit Citation	award presented by the President of the United States to US military units for outstanding performance. Also occasionally awarded to foreign units
RAAF	Royal Australian Air Force

reconnaissance	inspection of land or sea, usually abbreviated to 'recon'
roger	'yes' or 'I acknowledge'
round	bullet
Royal Marine Commandos	commando unit of the British Navy's Royal Marines
RP	rendezvous point or meeting place
SEALs (sea, air, land)	US Navy's Special Forces unit
seek on	a handler's instruction to an EDD to find explosives
SF-100	respirator/breathing device used by Special Forces as protection against nuclear, biological and chemical threats
SIG Sauer	German 9mm semi-automatic pistol; the P226 model is used by the US Navy SEALs
SOCOM	Special Operations Command
Special Air Service Regiment (SASR)	elite Special Forces unit in the Australian Army
Special Boat Service (SBS)	special operations unit of Britain's Royal Navy, specialising in small boat ops
Special Operations Engineer Regiment (SOER)	Australian Special Forces unit that specialises in military engineering and that trains and operates EDDs

special ops	special operations or secret missions
squadron	a small unit of Special Forces soldiers in the SAS; in the armies, air forces and navies of the world, the primary operational aircraft unit, often made up of a dozen aircraft or helicopters
Texas Rangers	formed in 1835 as a Texas police force, it is now a small law enforcement agency which focuses on major criminal cases
trooper	lowest rank in the SASR, the equivalent of a private in other army units
U-2	high altitude US surveillance aircraft with a crew of one
USAF	United States Air Force
USP	Heckler & Koch semi-automatic pistol, available in a variety of gauges
VC	Victoria Cross for Australia, the highest-ranking Australian military medal for gallantry
yomp	forced march with full equipment
zero hour	the time set down by military for an operation to begin

FACT FILE

Notes from the Author

If you have read the first book in this series, *Caesar the War Dog*, you will know that a real war dog named Caesar served with Anzac troops during the First World War (1914–18). That Caesar, a New Zealand bulldog, searched for wounded men and carried water to them. Another war dog named Caesar, a black labrador–kelpie cross, served with Australian forces during the Vietnam War as an Australian Army tracker dog.

A war dog named Caesar also served with US forces on the island of Bougainville during the Second World War, as the US President points out in this book.

The fictional Caesar in this book is based on several real dogs of modern times – Sarbi, Endal and Cairo – and their exploits. Here are a few more facts about the real dogs, people, military units, places and equipment that appear in this book and inspired the stories in this series.

EXPLOSIVE DETECTION DOGS (EDDs)

The Australian Imperial Force used dogs during the First World War, primarily to carry messages. Sarbi was preceded by a long line of sniffer dogs used by the Australian Army to detect land mines during the Korean War (1950–53) and, later, in the Vietnam War. In 1981, the current explosive detection dog program was introduced by the army's Royal Australian Engineer Corps, whose base is adjacent to Holsworthy Army Barracks in New South Wales. In 2005, Australian EDDs were sent to Afghanistan for the first time. A number have served there since and several have been killed or wounded in action.

SARBI

Sarbi, whose service number is EDD 436, is a black female labrador serving with the Australian Army. She began the EDD training program in June 2005 and graduated from the nineteen-week training course with Corporal D, joining the Australian Army's top-secret Incident Response Regiment (IRR) – now the Special Operations Engineer Regiment (SOER) – whose main job was to counter terrorist threats. In 2006, Sarbi and Corporal D were part of the security team at the Commonwealth Games in Melbourne. In April 2007, the pair was sent to Afghanistan for a seven-month deployment, returning to Afghanistan for their second tour of duty the following year.

On 2 September 2008, Sarbi and Corporal D were members of a Special Forces operation launched from a forward operating base a hundred kilometres northeast of Tarin Kowt. The operation went terribly wrong when five Humvees carrying Australian, American and Afghan troops were ambushed by a much larger Taliban force. In the ensuing battle, Corporal D was seriously wounded and became separated from Sarbi, who was also injured. Nine of the twelve Australians involved were wounded, as was their Afghan interpreter. Several American soldiers were also wounded in the battle. So began Sarbi's time lost in Taliban territory, a saga imagined in the first book of the Caesar the War Dog series.

After being 'missing in action' for thirteen months, Sarbi was wrangled back into friendly hands by a US Special Forces soldier. A month later, Sarbi and Corporal D were reunited at Tarin Kowt, in front of the Australian Prime Minister and the commanding US general in Afghanistan. Sarbi is the most decorated dog in the history of the Australian military, having been awarded all the medals that Caesar receives in *Caesar the War Dog*.

ENDAL

Endal was a sandy-coloured male labrador who was trained by the UK charity Canine Partners. He went on to qualify as a service dog and, in the late 1990s, was partnered with Allen Parton, a former Chief Petty Officer with Britain's Royal Navy. Confined to a wheelchair from injuries sustained during the Gulf War, initially Allen couldn't speak, so he taught Endal more than a hundred commands using hand signals.

In 2009, Endal suffered a stroke and had to be put down. During his lifetime, Endal became famous in Britain, receiving much media coverage and many awards for his dedicated and loyal service to his master. A young labrador named EJ (Endal Junior) took Endal's place as Allen Parton's care dog.

CAIRO

Cairo is a long-nosed Belgian Malinois shepherd with the United States Navy SEALs (Sea, Air and Land teams), a unit within the US Special Operations Command. He was trained for insertion by helicopter, and by parachute, strapped to his handler, just like Caesar is in this book. In 2011, Cairo was part of SEAL Team 6, which landed by helicopter in a compound in Pakistan to deal with Osama bin Laden, the leader of the terrorist organisation Al Qaeda. Cairo's job was to go in first to locate explosives in the compound. Cairo and all members of his team returned safely from the successful mission.

SPECIAL AIR SERVICE REGIMENT (SASR)

The original Special Air Service was created by the British Army during the Second World War for special operations behind enemy lines, with the motto of 'Who Dares Wins'. In 1957, the Australian Army created its own Special Air Service Regiment, commonly referred to as the Australian SAS, two years after the New Zealand Army founded its Special Air Service.

Australia's SAS is considered by many to be the finest Special Forces unit in the world, and its members help train Special Forces of other countries, including those of the United States of America.

The top-secret regiment is based at Campbell Barracks at Swanbourne, in Perth, Western Australia. Because its men are often involved in covert anti-terrorist work, their names and faces cannot be revealed. The only exceptions to this rule are SAS members who receive the Victoria Cross. The unit is divided into three squadrons, with one squadron always on anti-terrorist duty and the others deployed on specific missions.

During the war in Afghanistan, Australian EDDs and their handlers have frequently worked with Australian SAS and commando units on special operations.

ZOOMERS

Charlie's high-tech Zoomers are based on real prosthetic 'blades' used by athletes.

MEXICO AND THE FIGHT AGAINST CRIME CARTELS

A number of heavily armed criminal cartels do exist in Mexico, and they carry out the sort of crimes described in this book including murders, kidnapping, extortion and drug running. Whole towns and suburbs of major cities in Mexico have come under cartel control.

In the mid-2000s the Mexican Government reformed the Mexican Federal Police and deployed its army, navy and air force in an effort to wipe out the cartels and battle corruption within the police force. In this way the government has been successful in capturing and imprisoning a number of cartel leaders and driving cartels from some areas after major gun battles. But the struggle against the cartels continues.

The cartel names Àrbol and Estrella have been invented by the author, but the real cartels have similar names. The breakout of cartel members from Apodaca Prison in Nuevo León referred to in this book actually occurred in 2012.

THE UNITED NATIONS (UN)

The United Nations was founded in 1945 and its headquarters is situated in New York City, USA. To date it has 193 member states, including Australia, which fund its worldwide humanitarian and peacekeeping operations. The secretary-general, who is elected by its members, is the organisation's most senior officer.

Member states provide the UN's peacekeeping forces. UN humanitarian agencies include the United Nations Educational, Scientific and Cultural Organization (UNESCO), the World Health Organization (WHO), the World Food Programme (WFP), the International Court of Justice (ICJ or World Court), and the United Nations Children's Fund (UNICEF). Australia is currently a member of the UN Security Council, a body tasked with maintaining international peace and security.

About the Author

Stephen Dando-Collins is the award-winning author of more than thirty books, many of which have been translated into numerous languages. Most of Stephen's books are about military history and include subjects such as ancient Rome, the American West, colonial Australia, the First World War and the Second World War. *Pasteur's Gambit* was shortlisted for the science prize in the Victorian Premier's Literary Awards and won the Queensland Premier's Science Award. *Crack Hardy*, his most personal history, received wide acclaim. He has also written several titles for children and teenagers, including *Chance in a Million*, the Caesar the War Dog series and *Tank Boys*. Stephen and his wife, Louise, live and write in a former nunnery in Tasmania's Tamar Valley.

For more on other books by Stephen Dando-Collins, including books about Australian, American, British and ancient Roman and Greek military history, go to www.stephendandocollins.com

The first time that Corporal Ben Fulton saw Caesar, he didn't think much of him. In fact, he walked by him twice without a second glance. When he finally came to a stop in front of Caesar, on his third inspection of the line of dogs, Ben had a perplexed look on his face. 'That has got to be ugliest labrador retriever I have ever seen,' he said.

Corporal Ben had come to Huntingdon Kennels to look for a new dog, one that he could train to become an Australian Army sniffer dog. Huntingdon Kennels raised dogs for use by the police, emergency services and military, and Ben had asked to see the kennels' labrador retrievers. In his experience, labradors made the best sniffer dogs. So, the kennels lined up a dozen young labradors for Ben to inspect. Some were sandy coloured, some were black, and some, like Caesar, were brown. They were all aged between eighteen months and three years, and they sat in a line like soldiers, facing Ben. All had been given obedience training by the kennels.

As a result, they sat still and quiet as Ben walked up and down the line accompanied by Jan, a young woman who helped run the kennels.

Ben was looking for a dog with something special. The animal he ended up choosing would spend the rest of his working days with Ben, and there would be times when Ben's life, and the lives of other soldiers around them, would depend on that dog. So, Ben had to be sure that he and the dog would get on well, and that the animal had what it took to be a war dog. Just as every man doesn't always make a good soldier, not every dog has the courage, strength and loyalty to be a good war dog. None of the dogs Ben had viewed that morning stood out. Except for Caesar – and he stood out for all the wrong reasons – with his snout puffed up like a balloon on one side, he was not a pretty sight.

'That's Caesar,' said Jan. 'He's always getting into mischief. He went and stuck his nose into a beehive and got stung on the nose three or four times. The swelling will go down in a day or two. It doesn't seem to have bothered him much.'

As the corporal studied him, the labrador returned his gaze, taking in this well-built soldier of average height with a round, open face and dark, short-cropped hair. Then Caesar lowered his head, almost as if he was embarrassed by his puffy nose.

Ben smiled broadly. 'Poor Caesar,' he said, kneeling

beside the sitting dog and rubbing him behind the ear, which dogs love. 'Those nasty bee stings would have hurt like hell. Didn't they, mate?'

Caesar, immediately taking a liking to him, responded by wagging his tail and trying to lick Ben's face.

The manager of the kennels now joined them. 'You're not thinking of taking Caesar, are you, Corporal?' he said. 'That would be the worst dog in the kennels. We were considering getting rid of him.'

'Why?' Ben asked, turning to look at him.

'Caesar's always sticking his nose where he shouldn't,' said the manager. 'And he's a digger, too. Some dogs love to dig holes, but labrador retrievers aren't usually that interested in digging. This labrador would dig all day if you let him, just to see what he could dig up. That's not good for a working dog. You want his full attention.'

Ben patted Caesar's shining chocolate-brown coat, then stood up. He looked down at Caesar, and Caesar looked back up at him with a wagging tail and gleaming eyes that seemed to say, *Take me!*

'You know what?' said Ben. 'I'll take him, I'll take Caesar. I like him.'

'Really? Why him, of all dogs?' the surprised manager responded.

'Curiosity,' said Ben. 'A dog that puts his nose into a beehive and digs to see what he can find has loads of curiosity. And in my job, that's just the sort of dog

I need. He's got to be curious enough to find out what's hidden in a package, or to locate explosives hidden in a culvert beside the road. A dog like that can save lives.'

The manager shook his head. 'Well, good luck with him, Corporal. But I don't think you'll find Caesar will be much use to the army.'

'What's his ancestry?' Ben asked.

'His father and mother are labradors,' said Jan. 'But his grandfather was a German shepherd.'

'A German shepherd?' said Ben, nodding approvingly. 'I thought I could see a hint of another breed in his long snout. German shepherds are even more intelligent than labradors. If this dog has the best qualities of the curious labrador and the smart German shepherd, we could make quite a team.'

'Please yourself,' said the manager, unconvinced. 'But don't blame me if he disappoints you and lets you down one day.'

Despite the manager's lack of confidence in this brown labrador, Corporal Ben had been working with military dogs for ten years, and he considered himself the best judge. Signing the necessary papers, Ben officially made Caesar a recruit of the Australian Army, and made him his new trainee war dog.

STEPHEN DANDO-COLLINS

CAESAR

the war dog

operation
blue dragon

AVAILABLE NOW

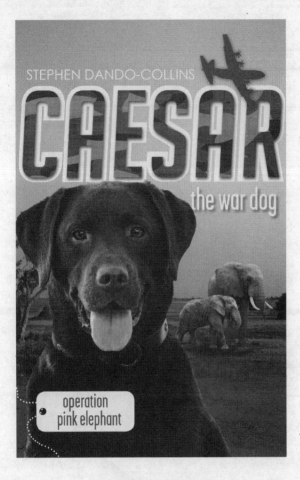

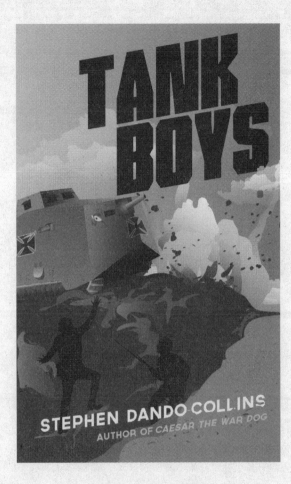

TANK BOYS

STEPHEN DANDO COLLINS
AUTHOR OF CAESAR THE WAR DOG

AVAILABLE NOW

Loved the book?

There's so much more
stuff to check out online

AUSTRALIAN READERS:

randomhouse.com.au/kids

NEW ZEALAND READERS:

randomhouse.co.nz/kids